SIMON FRENCH began his writing career as a thirteen year old in Sydney's western suburbs, and had his first novel published five years later while still at high school.

In the years since, his writing for children has earned critical acclaim and several awards, including the 1987 Children's Book Council of Australia's Book of the Year award for *All We Know*.

The characters in his stories often develop from the children he has worked with—from babies and toddlers in an inner-city crisis refuge, to the pupils he has taught over many years at primary schools in suburban and rural New South Wales. Simon continues to work as a teacher in a small school in Sydney's rural outskirts.

He is unable to imagine life without good books, interesting music and movies, exotic food, travel to new places, old cars—but, most of all, true friends.

Where in the World

SIMON FRENCH

LITTLE 🐇 HARE

Published by Little Hare Books
45 Cooper Street, Surry Hills
NSW 2010 AUSTRALIA

First published in 2002
Reprinted in 2002

National Library of Australia
Cataloguing-in-Publication entry

French, Simon, 1957– .
    Where in the world.

    For children aged 10 years and older.
    ISBN 1 877003 03 4.

    1. Boys — Australia — Juvenile fiction. 2. Family —
Juvenile fiction. 3. Music — Juvenile fiction. I. Title.

A823.3

Cover illustration by Vivienne Goodman
Cover design by ANTART
Set in 12.5/16.5 Bembo by Asset Typesetting Pty Ltd
Printed and bound in Australia by McPherson's Printing Group

5 4 3 2

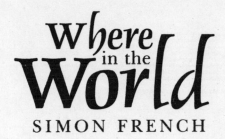

Where in the World

SIMON FRENCH

SOMEWHERE ELSE

So there *was* something that made Thomas scared.

It wasn't expected and I hadn't meant it to happen. I'd only wanted to show him the lookout.

"You've never seen it before?" I asked.

"No."

"What about the caves?"

"No."

"But you've lived here longer than me, and these places are so close to where you live. What about the walking track to the waterfalls?"

"My parents don't take me to places like that," Thomas replied. "They don't like bushwalking. It's like hard work to them, and they'd worry about snakes and other bitey stuff."

"What about when you go on holidays, what do you do then?"

"We stay at resorts and just ... hang around.

You know, swim in the pool or go to the games room or something."

His answers surprised me a lot. "When we first moved here," I said, "we went exploring. Did the walk to the falls, went out to the caves. And this lookout, it's only a short walk from my place. I've come here about a hundred times and—"

And I realised I was talking to myself. At the end of the walking path, where the safety fence finished, I found myself alone, with the cold air from the valley breezing up at my face. Thomas had stopped a short way behind.

"What is it?" I asked. "What's up?"

"Nothing," he said, but in a voice that told me: *something*.

"It's a great view, you should see it. Sometimes there are wallabies on the other side. This valley is way deep. When my mum first saw it she said, Now that's what I call a hole in the ground. Except of course she said it in German and— Are you coming to look?"

But Thomas shook his head, and suddenly he was sitting on the path. The look on his face was as though he'd seen something awful, or had woken from a bad dream. And then I began to understand. "Hey, it's okay. There's a fence; you won't fall. Thomas?"

I could tell he wasn't about to come any closer. So I walked the few steps back, sat down next to him and tried to read the look on his face. This wasn't the Thomas I was used to, my best friend who told good jokes and said things that made kids and teachers laugh.

"I can see fine from here," he said. But from where we sat, there was no view at all.

"It's heights," he said at last. "I hate being high up. I feel like I'm going to fall, or be pushed. And I get dizzy and sick. I don't know why, it just happens."

I thought about this a moment. "Sorry, I didn't bring you here to scare you. I just wanted to show you."

Thomas nodded slowly, picked up a stick and drew patterns in the dirt.

"I didn't think I'd like flying in a plane," I told him. "The first time we came over from Germany it was just for a holiday, and my cousin Anya told me I'd probably be airsick because she'd done nothing but spew up the first time she went on a plane. Then, when Mum and I were first on board, there was a safety demonstration about lifejackets and emergency exits, and that made me nervous, too."

"And was it that bad?" Thomas asked. "Did you get airsick?"

I shook my head. "Once we were in the air, it was great. I loved it."

Thomas nodded, but kept drawing his dirt patterns.

"There were other kids on the plane," I said,

"and the cabin crew invited a group of us up to the cockpit to meet the pilots. Back where the passengers were it was kind of noisy and busy. But in the cockpit it was really still and quiet." I paused then, not sure if I was talking too much.

"That'd be weird," Thomas said.

"Yeah, it was. But the view out the cockpit windows was the best bit. The horizon, it wasn't straight, the way it looks when you're at the beach and you see it over the ocean. It was like this ..." And Thomas watched as I drew the shape in the air with an outstretched arm and finger. "It was curved."

"Curved?"

"You could see the shape of the planet."

And I could see it all again in my head now—blue sky, blue ocean, curved horizon. When I closed my eyes, the still of the bush and the cool air from the valley could have matched how it felt standing in the cockpit all that time ago.

Until the minute that Thomas asked quietly, "Can we go back now?", I was somewhere else. Flying, floating, remembering. I remembered everything.

LONG AGO AND FAR AWAY

"Das ist Talent," Opa had said to my mother. *This is talent.*

"Was ist das?" I had asked. *Talent, what's that?*

"Schlau," he replied. *Clever.* Copying my violin notes so accurately. Understanding all these dots and squiggles on a music sheet so quickly.

Opa, grandfather.

Mama, Illona, Mum.

When Thomas asked me to speak German, "Opa" at least sounded familiar to him. He giggled about the other word.

"Mama," he joked. "Mama, mama. Like a talking doll."

"Yeah, Thomas, very funny, ha ha. It's an old joke and I've heard it before, you know. Anyway, I don't call her that any more. I just say 'Mum'. Honest."

But that whole other way of saying things stayed

in my head, kept for speaking at particular times. Like when the relatives called us long-distance, or for a once-in-a-while conversation with Mum. Sometimes I'd wake up and remember a dream spoken in German, but everything I thought about when I was awake was in English. Even when it was about my father.

Emil, father, Dad.

My dad lived in a small photo.

He wore a bright jumper and a leather jacket. He smiled a broad smile. In the photo, I was a tiny boy who rode behind him in a baby backpack. I wore a scarf, woolly mittens and a cap, and I smiled like my dad.

Mum told me we had been on a trip to Berlin, for a peace rally, when she had photographed the two of us, our faces and smiles in a sea of strangers.

He had taken a companion photo of her in the same crowd, but that photo lived in an album that showed my parents together and me aged one, two and three.

The two copies of the photo of me and my dad lived separately in two silver frames, which were decorated with patterns of thistles—one my mum kept in her bedroom; the other I kept in mine, on my bedside table. My dad smiled at me from a distant place and I tried to imagine what it might have been like riding in the baby backpack or hearing his voice.

"Do you ever miss him?" I asked Mum once.

"Ari, I think about him every day. How about you?"

I shrugged. "I wish he was still alive." In the same voice, I could have said, *I wish the sun would shine today*, and I worried that the way I'd said it would sound like I didn't care.

But Mum told me, "If he was still alive today, he'd be very proud of you."

So I knew she still missed my father, sometimes enough for both of us.

I had two things of his—a silver watch with a revolving picture on its face of the sun and the moon, each showing themselves for day or night, and the brocade vest I wore on Fridays and Saturdays in our cafe. Mum explained that my dad had admired the one Opa wore, which Opa had bought in India when he had gone travelling as a young man. So Opa found a similar one at the markets in Göttingen and gave it to my dad as a gift.

"Now you can be an old hippy like me, is what your Opa said to your dad," Mum told me. "They got on well together, Emil and Opa. Always joking around with each other."

Where did he go? Why doesn't he come back?

I thought I could remember asking those

7

questions about my dad, and I must have, because eventually I understood the answer Mum gave me.

He left for work earlier than usual one Friday. It was two weeks after you'd turned three, and there was a computer problem at his office that he needed to sort out by the weekend. It was still dark, and raining, too. There was a major accident on the road, lots of cars with lots of people hurt. And Emil, your dad, was one who didn't make it.

I was five when I understood that answer and had thought about it ever since, but I never asked Mum about it again. Instead, I wanted to know, "Am I like my dad was?"

Mum could answer that one with a bit of a smile. "He was really good at maths, just like you are. A marvel with computers. He loved music, too, but couldn't play an instrument to save himself. He could sing, though. He had a nice voice. He was a good person, Ari."

"Like Jamie?"

She considered this. "In some ways, they're quite the same. In other ways, quite different."

Jamie. James Nicol. Jamie.

"I'm not about to try to replace your dad," he told me once. "I'm just here to be me. Someone you can talk to whenever, about whatever."

And I nodded a quiet reply, because I

appreciated him putting it like that. But there was an odd, sharp pain as well; I blinked hard and thought of the thistle-framed photo.

We were bushwalking in a place Jamie knew from long ago. The hills were pockmarked with old gold diggings; there was ancient machinery, a convict road and the honey-sweet smell of wattle blossom. Mum strode ahead the way she often did when we went exploring.

"Does she always walk that fast?" Jamie asked.

"Always," I said. "I had to run to keep up when I was little."

"What's 'slow down' in German? Give her a yell, Ari."

"Hey Mum," I called to the figure disappearing over the next hill. "Mach langsam!"

"You've lost a bit of your accent, you know," Mum had remarked once or twice. "When you speak, I can hear a difference. Like those vapour trails that jets leave in the sky … gradually they disappear. Maybe one day you'll simply sound like a little Aussie." *Ossy*, she pronounced it.

In the week or two, long ago, that I'd been the new boy at school, the other kids giggled whenever I said something.

Hey Ari, it sounds funny, the way you talk.

Hey Ari, tell us some rude words in German.

Hey Ari, how do you say "Mr Manning is a dag"?

But other new kids had arrived in the months that followed, so now I was just me: Ari, who's a good goalie at soccer. Ari, who always finishes his maths work before anybody else. Ari, who lives out of town, at that cafe near the caves.

It was the customers at the cafe who asked me now, the people who visited for the first time. When I said hello and took them to their table, they'd hear the accent in my voice and ask, "And where are you from?"

From Hattorf, in Germany. We came here for a holiday when I was eight, and liked it so much we came back again to live. I've lived here nearly three years. My mum and stepfather do the food. We stop serving meals at nine-thirty. If you stay past then, you get to hear some music. Yes, that's the stage over there. My mum and stepfather do the music. And Allison and Ben, they're uni students. They play piano and double bass. No, I don't go on stage—I watch. Would you like your wine put in the fridge? I can do that. And someone will be out soon to take your order. Yes, I like living here—it's fun. My name's Ari.

OUTSIDE

I liked the sound of my violin outside.

It echoed against the back wall of the house and sounded clear and loud in the silence of the cafe garden. I did my music practice outside as often as possible—seven days a week, for half an hour, maybe forty-five minutes at a time. It made my fingers sore and my shoulders ache a bit, but I hardly ever had to be reminded or nagged to go practise by Mum or Jamie. Though sometimes they had other things to say.

It's too cold. It'll be dark soon. It's too hot. Won't the wind blow your music sheets all over the garden?

But I liked the outdoors. I liked the flow of the music I was good at, and I liked to work on mistakes without anyone else nearby. I played scales, warm-ups, excerpts and complete pages of music score. Some scales could be as easy as walking up and down stairs, others could be like working my way through a complicated obstacle course.

Practise, Mr Lee always reminded me, timing, accuracy, expression, concentration. The first thing I always did was work through the homework he set me each week, until I could nearly play it without looking at the music score.

But just as I always had my music homework folder outside to work from, I also had at least one of the primers Opa had made for me. Some he had given to me when I was little, but most of the others he had put together and then mailed; they had arrived in fat envelopes with "Ari Huber, violinist" written as the address in Opa's swirling handwriting.

They were like scrapbooks, filled with photocopies of music from his books, sometimes an exercise or score written in his own hand. Always the things he had loved playing, and always with little comments he had added. Whenever I read these, it was not a lesson, but the sort of conversation we might have had together.

Mozart, *Eine Kleine Nachtmusik*, A little night music. *Als ich Zehn war*, When I was ten, Ari, I learned this. You're bound to be taught it by someone else, but here it is from me. It's still a favourite of mine to play, even after all these years.

Schwebend, floating. That's how this excerpt by

Holst should begin. Think of yourself among the stars and planets in outer space, and wonder about how quiet and how vast the universe is.

Das ist Volksmusik. This is folk music. Long before rock and roll, there were plenty of other great tunes to dance and get silly to. This piece, "The Hens' March", is from England. Lots of quick, dancing notes—the ones written in blue are the hens squawking, so make your violin squawk, too. Drive your mother crazy! Enjoy!

From photos and things remembered, I knew that music and Opa had always belonged together. But it was only after Mum had packed away my father's belongings and moved herself and me to Opa's farm that I really knew and understood. That the orchestra had been his life, but there had come a time to leave. That he had given up rehearsals, touring and concerts, but could never give up music.

This is your home for as long as you want, he had said to my mother. As long as you can still put up with classical music for at least a couple of hours each day.

So in the moments when I wasn't being Opa's second shadow, or making roads in his gardens for my toy cars or chasing his pet goats, I knew I could always find him by following the direction the music was coming from. If it wasn't from his stereo in the lounge room, it would be the sound of his violin from the backyard. And that was how it began.

When I played in the orchestra, he told me, it was nearly always indoors. I've had a lifetime indoors; I want to be outdoors now.

His favourite spot was a seat in the garden behind the house. If the weather was kind, he'd be out there most days, playing his favourite music with nothing else but his violin and his memory.

He taught me to play, too, pleased when I'd first shown interest, and then surprised when he saw how quickly I got to know my tiny learners' violin, that I could soon follow his notes and make my way through his music score sheets.

This is wonderful, he'd say to Mum. But he needs more than I can give.

Nonsense, she had replied. Ari will never have a more valuable teacher. He'll learn things from you he'll always remember.

Outside. If I closed my eyes, I could see every shape in Opa's garden. I could still remember the names of his pet goats. I could still see him sitting on the garden seat playing music.

And now I was being called inside.

The afternoon silence had been gradually replaced with sounds. Somewhere in the background, I'd heard Allison arriving for work. There had been the clockwork chug of her VW, a door opening and closing, and her cheery "Hi everybody!" Someone had put a tape or CD into the cafe sound system and from the open window of the kitchen came the first sounds of food preparation—laughter and conversation, the clatter of baking trays, my mum suddenly singing some lines from a song, loudly and happily. "Ari! Show time!" she called then.

I ignored her for a minute or two more, flipping open the music primer I had brought outside and finding the page where Opa had pasted the piece of music by Holst.

"Jupiter, the Bringer of Jollity," I murmured to myself. "Schwebend, floating. Think of yourself among the stars and planets."

The cafe garden was completely in shadow, and I could feel the first of the evening's cool against my face. Holst was my last piece of music for now and, as I began to play, someone inside turned the stereo down.

Even before I reached the final note, I knew they were all up there, watching and listening. As I held the bow away from my violin to let the last sound float away, I heard cheers and applause. They were all at the open window, leaning on the sill—Mum, Jamie, Ben, and Allison, with her brightly coloured hair and crazy earrings.

"Hi Ari," Allison called. "That sounded so nice."

Jamie gave a thumbs-up and called, "Encore!"

Mum shook her head. "You play Holst very nicely, Ari. But it's time to come in. Time for jobs."

I carefully set my violin back in its case, unwound the bow a little and packed it away, too. And closed the pages of my primer.

Schön gespielt, Ari, is what Opa might have said. *Nicely played*.

I went inside.

IN THE CAR

Each Friday, Jamie saved me having to ride home in the school bus, so I didn't have to put up with the noisy high schoolers who always took up the back seats, or the kindergarten kids who picked their noses every five minutes when they thought no one was looking.

On Fridays, Jamie would park on the street near the school gates, and would usually be reading a newspaper when I opened the car door to get in. Friday was his half-day tutoring music at the uni, and it was also shopping day for the cafe. The back of the station wagon would always be packed with boxes of vegetables and herbs, an esky full of pastry sheets and dairy stuff, a tray of breads ... The front seat was definitely the only place I could hope to fit. The whole inside of the car smelled of food, and it was like riding home in a giant shopping trolley.

"So how was your day?" Jamie asked, folding his newspaper away and turning the car's ignition key.

"Good," I answered, which was my usual reply once my nose had adjusted to garlic and vegetables.

"Terrific-good or average-good?"

"Average-good."

Jamie worked his way through end-of-school traffic and onto the main street, glancing at me long enough to say, "Well, come on—more detail."

"We had a maths test—easy. We had Friday assembly—boring. We did sport and played Mr Brock's class in soccer—"

"Win, lose or draw?"

"Three one, our loss."

"Ha! Doesn't your class usually win?"

"The kids in Mr Brock's class are all giants. And Mr Brock was reffing and let his kids off on fouls twice and—"

"It sounds completely tragic. What if Ms Orton had refereed instead?"

"Then we would have won," I said, but Jamie started laughing. "We would have! Ms Orton's really fair."

"Not biased like Mr Brock?"

"No way."

"Any homework this weekend?"

"Just my science project for Monday. And music practice."

"How are the music lessons going?"

"Okay, but—"

"But what?"

"Mr Lee told me on Wednesday that he's going to organise all his violin pupils to put on an end-of-year performance. He's going to send parents a note about it."

"That sounds all right."

I shook my head. "He wants to put me with seven other kids, all older than me. High school kids. And he wants me to do a solo piece as well."

"That's probably to do with how well you play."

"But I'll be the youngest. And we'd be playing to everybody's families—parents, grandparents, brothers, sisters, aunts, uncles."

"So there might be a big audience. You don't like that?"

"No."

"But you've played in front of an audience before —and how about when you've gone for your violin grades? That's only a handful of people, but remember your last grade exam? It was tough stuff. Wouldn't an end-of-year performance for some parents be a snap?"

I didn't reply.

"It's a few months away yet," Jamie said. "You shouldn't be getting worried about it, Ari."

We came to the traffic lights at the end of the main street and turned onto the highway, leaving the shops in town behind. Gradually, the ridges where the houses were became hills and valleys of bush, until our own turn-off came into view.

"We need a sign at this corner," Jamie said, half to himself. "Mayfair Cafe, fine food and fabulous music. Or fabulous food and fine music? Something like that." He blinked his eyes and gave his head a shake, as though he was just waking up.

"What is it?' I asked.

"This moment in time. Here in the car. Me, driving an eleven year old home from school. Talking about things."

"It's what we do," I replied. "It happens every week."

"Sure," Jamie said. "But a few years ago I could never have imagined I'd be here. I didn't even want to be a parent, let alone a step-parent."

I felt alarmed. "Why not?"

"Because as far as I was concerned back then, all kids were smelly, noisy, hungry, expensive, revolting little creatures."

"Thanks a lot!"

"No, not you. That's just it. When I first met you

and your mum, I was expecting to discover you had a revolting side—that you threw tantrums or had other bad habits. But I've been nicely surprised. So far."

"Thank you," I said, not sure whether to laugh or feel embarrassed.

"Just as long as you don't turn into the teenager from hell in a few years time," Jamie added in a warning voice.

"I'll try not to. Maybe."

The tourist sign to the caves came into view, and then the last curve in the road before our cafe.

"Home," Jamie said. "You know, I think of tutoring at the uni as a job. But even though we work hard here at the cafe, it never really feels like work to me. It feels like home. I always thought I'd miss living in cities, but I don't." He changed gears to slow down, and glanced at me. "Is there any place you ever miss being, Ari?"

I shrugged, but then nodded. "Yeah. Sometimes."

ON A TRAIN

aged 6

Where were we?

On the floor in Opa's lounge room, with a large map unfolded and spread like a picnic rug.

When your papa and I went travelling, Mama told me, we went this way. And she traced a line over the colours and writing. The Netherlands, Belgium, France, Spain, Italy. Now, when you and I go travelling, we're going *this* way. From north to south. From rain and cold here in Hattorf, to sun and warmth on a Greek island. How does that sound to you, Ari?

What will we see?

Mountains higher than you can imagine. One of the longest railway tunnels in the world. An ancient city buried long ago by a volcanic eruption. Beautiful beaches and water as clear as window glass.

I put my face close to the map, and traced a railway line that led to Russia. Is Opa coming too?

No, it's just you and me. Your Opa has made a gift of two holiday rail passes. We're very lucky.

Holiday. From the backyard, their kitchen conversations had drifted out to me through open windows, had echoed up the staircase to my bedroom at night.

Opa's voice: A real holiday, Illona. Go travelling with your friends the way you used to.

Mama's voice: Most of my friends are married or overseas. You know I don't see anyone much any more.

Opa's voice: I've seen you work so hard at your studies, at being a parent. You've hidden yourself away here too long—some time away would do you the world of good. You know Ari can stay with me.

Mama's voice: I know. But I'm not ready to be apart from him just yet. So if I go, Ari comes with me.

Where were we?

In Opa's car, driving to the railway station.

Our backpacks were in the boot. My fingers were in my mouth and I was staring at the raindrops spattering against the window.

Opa's voice: I'm still not sure how relaxing three weeks travelling across Europe with a six year old is going to be.

Mama's voice: Me either. No late-night parties, I guess.

And through the gap between the front seats, I saw her take the hand that Opa had lifted away from the steering wheel.

"Du zitterst," he told her. *You're trembling.*

"Ich weiss," she replied. *I know.* Suddenly, this all feels a bit strange.

Opa nodded slowly before putting his hand back on the steering wheel.

In the carpark at the station, he not only pulled our big and little packs from the boot, but my small violin in its case as well.

Mama said, So I'm to have a musical holiday, am I?

She wasn't exactly pleased, and was worried that the violin would be lost or stolen, even though there was a strap and little padlock that secured it to my backpack.

Opa laughed. I'm not having our clever musician here miss out on three weeks of violin practice. You'll find a little book of music in his bag.

He waited with us until the express train came slowly through the points and signals towards the platform. As it did, it seemed Opa was trying to fit a day's worth of talking into a minute.

Travel safely. Find somewhere decent to stay

each night. Ring me if you need anything. Have a wonderful trip.

He scooped me into his arms. And you have a fabulous holiday, too. Don't lose your mother, and don't forget to do some music practice.

At the door of the railway carriage Opa finally set me down, and my next view of him was through the window beside my seat. His muffled voice made him suddenly seem so far away.

The train bumped and began to move, and I pressed my face to the window glass so that my nose squashed flat. We were waving, all waving to each other until the platform came to an end and Opa's face and shape grew smaller, more distant, and then was lost from view.

I told Mama that I thought Opa looked sad.

He's going to miss playing music with his favourite violinist, she replied.

We're coming back though, aren't we? I wanted to know.

Of course we are, she said. But you know, Ari, we won't be living at the farm forever.

Where were we?

When I looked ahead, there was the back of a seat, its net pocket stuffed with magazines and an empty drink cup. The window near me was a mirror reflection because outside was night-dark, and no landscape could be seen. The reflection showed where *I* was—seats, luggage and other people. When I arched my head backwards on Mama's lap, I could see the teenagers across the aisle, still awake and playing a card game. When I looked straight above, Mama was asleep. Her mouth was open a little, and a coil of her dreadlocked hair tickled against my forehead. I was stretched across my seat and hers; it wasn't as comfortable as my own bed.

Click, click–click, went the railway beat below.

"Mama," I said softly, "Mama, wach auf." *Wake up.*

When her eyes opened for a moment, they were sky-blue and blurry. "Hallo," she murmured in a faraway voice. And closed her eyes again.

The train shuddered a little, snapped over points, and raced past the lights and doors of a railway station.

"Mama," I said again, and she groaned and stretched like one of Opa's lazy cats.

Ari, what is it?

The sounds around me were so different to home—the train, the teenagers and their card-game talk, the man in the seat behind us snoring, and the faint *tsh-tsh* of music in someone's headphones.

Mama opened her eyes wide and looked at me carefully. Are you okay? she asked quietly.

I nodded slowly. Outside our carriage was a

black and unknown place. I could have asked Mama where we were, except she was already closing her eyes for more sleep. My hand found one of hers, and I held tightly. Her other hand moved to wipe the hair from my forehead, and she stroked my head as the train beat click, click-click, beneath us.

In the darkness of the night before, in my bedroom at Opa's, she had done much the same.

In my head now, I heard the voice that had told me: Ari, you try to get some sleep. Tomorrow, our adventures begin.

NUREMBERG

aged 6

The train was late.

We were supposed to leave Nuremberg at
6.35pm and be checked in at the youth hostel in
Munich by nine, but instead a voice over the platform
loudspeaker said something that made the waiting
crowd groan and grumble.

What is it? I asked Mama. Is the train late?

"Sehr," she answered. *Very*. There's a problem
with the track signals somewhere. Everything is
delayed. We're going to miss our booking at the hostel.

My mother was at a loss. She sighed loudly, and
little white clouds of breath escaped from her mouth
into the darkness. It was cold.

Other people were around us. Their voices
complained and I heard other accents, other languages
being spoken. English I had heard often enough in

music and on TV, and Mama and Opa had taught me some simple things to say. I could answer to "What is your name? What is your mother's name? How old are you?" in case things ever went wrong when we travelled. And now I could hear plenty of English being spoken, people getting cranky with the railway staff about the late train.

"Isn't there another connecting train? Is there a bus we can get?" asked a young man. He had a sleepy face and hair that stuck out at every angle.

And I complained too. "Ich bin müde, Mama." *I'm tired.* I don't want to stay here. I'm cold. I said the last bit several times, "Mir ist kalt, mir is kalt," as my mother flicked through her youth hostel guide.

Ari, I'm thinking, I'm thinking, she said in a not-quite-patient voice.

I said it all over again, and this time she replied so loudly that everyone nearby on the platform turned for a moment and stared at us. I wasn't used to her being angry at me, and sat myself heavily on the seat between our backpacks and had a bit of a cry. I'd had enough of walking around old towns and old castles. I wanted a warm bed in a warm room. I wanted breakfast in the morning, sitting up at a proper table. We'd been catching trains for three days already, and I was fed up with trains. I wanted to be at home with Opa.

Finally, Mama sat beside me, and mopped my wet eyes and dribbly nose. She had her mobile phone out by now, was pressing numbers and having conversations about rooms for the night. Other travellers around us were doing much the same thing, and gradually they began leaving the platform, heaving backpacks and discussing hotels and taxis.

Everything I can afford is either booked out or too far away, my mother said, half to her mobile, half to me. And then she groaned because the phone battery was starting to die.

Ari, we simply may have to wait here until a train does arrive.

"Warum?" I asked. *Why?* What would Opa say?

Mama pulled a face. Ari, that's really the last thing I want to think about just now. She closed her eyes, shook her head slowly and put a hand up to her forehead as though a headache was coming.

When we stopped talking, I realised how quiet it had become all around us. Lots of people had left the platform by now. A few travellers were arranging their backpacks into cushions to lean against and nap, or else they were at the vending machines getting drinks or chocolates.

I got a taste in my mouth for chocolate as well, but decided not to risk asking. "Ich bin müde," I told Mama yet again.

I know you're tired, she replied, struggling to get another call through on her mobile.

"Mir ist kalt."

I know you're cold.

"Mir ist *sehr* kalt," I added. *Very*.

Mama gave up on her phone and turned to me. Come on, she said. Let's have a short walk and a change of scenery. Something more interesting to look at than train tracks. But close enough to be able to hear announcements about trains.

So we put on our backpacks and walked the short distance outside to the seats beside the taxi rank. We sat down.

We sat a long time, as the sky darkened to night and the town lights came on. There were no announcements from the railway loudspeakers about the train to Munich arriving soon.

Mama had unbuttoned her coat and wrapped it around me like a cocoon so that only my face showed.

I'm sorry this has happened, Ari, but it can't be helped. Maybe I forgot a little while ago that you're only six years old. I'm tired and a bit fed up, too, but you're the one who probably needs a sleep. So get warm and close your eyes for a bit.

I didn't, I began—and yawned a big yawn— I didn't do any violin practice today.

Never mind, Mama replied, and smiled a bit. You're too tired for that now. Some music practice tomorrow, okay? In the meantime, we wait for a train.

What if we have to wait all night? I was going to ask, but there was someone else's voice instead.

A man and his wife had walked over to where we sat and had begun talking to my mother. They were as grey-haired as Opa.

We closed our shop at seven o'clock, the man told Mama, and pointed at a window of books across the road. You were sitting here then and you're still here now. Are you travelling? Are you in a fix?

When Mama explained about the train problem, the man said, We live in the apartment above the bookshop. You and your little one need a bed for the night and we've a spare room. Come and stay with us. By morning the train problem should be sorted.

So I was given supper and put into a bed that smelled of lavender.

Mama and I woke up beside each other the next morning and had breakfast in the kitchen. There was a view from a big window onto a tiny backyard and a row of other shops and yards. The couple asked questions about my little violin and about our travelling.

You're a brave girl! the woman said to my mother. When the grandchildren are here to visit, I have enough adventures just taking them shopping.

Their grandchildren looked at us from photos on every wall and shelf top. I wondered which one would be the best fun to play with, but asked out loud, "Welches ist das frechste?" *Which one is the naughtiest?*

That made them laugh. "Felix!" they both agreed, and showed me a photo of a boy a little older than me. He wore a soccer shirt and had toothy gaps in his smile.

The grandparents wouldn't take any money from Mama, and they fussed over us exactly as Opa would have done. Before they opened their bookshop for the day, they walked us across to the railway station and waited with us until the train to Munich arrived.

You've got tears, I told Mama after the train had left Nuremberg. Why?

She reminded me of your grandmother, Ari. Just the way she said particular things.

Oh.

They thought we were running away, you know. That I had left a mean husband. At first they didn't believe you and I were travelling across Europe on a holiday. They told me you were one of the littlest backpackers they had ever seen.

They liked it when I played some violin, I said.

Mama nodded. They were kind and very trusting. I wish I could return the favour somehow.

Two weeks after we left the grandparents in Nuremberg, we sent postcards.

In the courtyard behind the youth hostel in Amsterdam, I did my violin practice while Mama wrote her postcard. Then, on a scrap of paper, she printed out the message I wanted to send so I could copy it onto my postcard.

In my best and smallest writing I said: Thank you for a warm bed and a nice breakfast. I would like to meet the naughtiest grandchild one day. From Ari Huber.

An e-mail, Friday afternoon

Opa, something unusual has started happening.

Every second Friday, when I'm doing music practice in the cafe garden, a car arrives outside and stops. Not anyone we know. Allison, who works in the kitchen, has a VW bug and you know what they sound like. And Ben, the double bass player, has a motorbike we can hear five kilometres away. This other car arrives really quietly. It's black—a Saab, Jamie says, because he's noticed it across the road, too. I've seen the car in town, but I've never seen the boy who sits in the car. He doesn't go to my school.

His mum is always with him. She never gets out of the car, but he does sometimes. To look up and down the road, to walk around—until his mum calls for him to get back in again. I call him the Friday Boy, because it's the only time I see him out there.

Mum said not to be a stickybeak. But near my

favourite practice spot in the cafe garden, there's a gap in the fence, and I can see nearly everything that's happening outside without even trying.

So I think I know a bit about the Friday Boy. That he lives with his mum and not his dad. That he gets to see his dad every second weekend. I know that because after a while a second car arrives and parks behind the black Saab. And when the boy climbs out of his mum's car, he's got a bag, a big overnight bag.

I've heard his voice. "Bye Mum, hi Dad." He drives away in his dad's car and the black Saab drives off in the other direction.

One time the parents got out of their cars and argued with each other, right in front of the boy. It sounded awful, so I picked up my violin and went inside. I didn't want to listen.

Another time I was outside practising and hadn't heard anybody arrive out the front. When I stopped to turn a page of the music, I heard the Friday Boy's voice say, "That's not a CD, that's someone really playing. A kid by the sound of it."

A kid! I quickly found and played the trickiest bit of Mozart I knew. Then I heard him say, "No, maybe it's a grown-up."

But I have to tell you what happened today. My fingers and arms were sore, and I was about to quit, when I thought of one more piece I wanted to play.

Something from one of the primers you sent me, book number seven. The Friday Boy was out there, standing next to his mum's car and looking down the road for his dad. I could see him, but he couldn't see me. "Hey," he said when I stopped playing, "that person across the road is playing the same Bach piece I've been learning."

I've never heard his parents say his name, so that's another reason why I think of him as the Friday Boy. I wouldn't like to be him, having two parents in two different houses. But maybe he wouldn't like to be me, either, standing at a kitchen sink washing dirt and slugs out of salad greens. And now Mum's calling, "Ari! Show time!', so I have to go. Bye, Opa.

NAPLES

aged 6

It felt dangerous in Naples.

There was the man in the smart suit, who told Mama he was an airline pilot but then tried to sell her an expensive watch, and followed us up and down streets until we managed to lose him.

There was the sweaty air that pushed through the open upstairs window at the youth hostel where we stayed and, later at night, the sounds of men fighting on the street below.

"Mir gefällt es hier nicht," I whispered to Mama when I'd left my bunk bed to cuddle up beside her. *I don't like it here.*

The day we walked along a road in the old part of town, a voice called to us in English, "Hey, you must be thirsty. Want some water?"

Mama said yes, because ours had turned warm in

the bottle inside her backpack. We saw a man, a woman and some children just inside the doorway of a little house. Once inside, the man lectured Mama about religion.

When Mama finally managed to leave, she was pulling a face as she came out the door. As we walked away through the back streets, she told me, They sold everything they owned, that family—their house, the car, the works—and moved here to Italy to be missionaries for their church. Those poor kids.

Why? I asked.

Ari, they don't even go to school. Those children have a little education at home, but otherwise they're out working—cleaning houses, running messages—to support the household. Can you imagine that?

But I couldn't at first, because I'd just spent some time kicking a ball in the street with the missionaries' kids.

Ari, people are quite amazing sometimes. The things they put their children through.

"Mir gefällt es hier nicht," I repeated. Can we go somewhere else?

This is travelling, Ari, Mama told me. Not always happy adventures, but sometimes you learn unexpected things about people and places. One day, you'll have lots of interesting stories to tell.

We finished up on a stretch of grass beside a busy

street near the youth hostel. My mother had retrieved my violin and lesson book from the locker at the hostel; she lay on the grass, tired from the day. I did my violin practice.

I did my scales, then worked through three or four little pieces Opa had written out for me, concentrating as hard as I could. But the daylight was starting to fade and I was tired from the day's walk as well. I felt a bit daydreamy, and Opa's musical notes blurred a little.

My mother had closed her eyes to listen to me, but now opened them suddenly and asked, What's that you're playing?

I don't know. I made it up.

Made it up? Ari, it's beautiful. Can you play it again?

I was thinking about that family, those kids, I tried to explain. Something I couldn't quite put into words made me a little sad. I played my made-up music some more.

Mama was sitting up now, watching me closely.

I've never heard you do that before, she said, making up your own tune. I should be writing the notes down as you play, so they won't be forgotten.

"Ich werde es nicht vergessen." *I won't forget.*

And I played my music again, this time adding a whole new section onto where I'd finished before.

Mama opened her eyes wide and smiled. Then, in a thoughtful, surprised voice, she said, "Mein schlauer Sohn." *My clever son.* Your Opa was right about you, and I can tell him so on our postcard from Naples.

"Ich habe Hunger," I said then. *I'm hungry.*

She laughed. Me too. I should have brought my guitar on this trip. We could have played music on a street corner and made ourselves some holiday spending money. Maybe next time … You play me five more minutes of your made-up music, then we'll go find somewhere with nice food, where we can sit outdoors and eat—and we'll watch the sun set.

The clouds in the sky were turning purple and orange, and there was so much traffic on the street beside us that all the cars had come to a stop. I turned the colours and sounds into music, a little of it the same as I'd just played, a little of it quite different again. Mama sat on the grass cross-legged, her eyes closed, her face smiling and her head bobbing slowly like waves on water.

I could see people in cars looking at us. One person leaned out of a car window and took a photo. I weaved the bow back and forth across the strings, realising I'd done something special.

And I'd turned a bad day into a good one. I didn't mind Naples so much now.

An e-mail, Saturday night

Show time.

Opa, when Mum says that, it's really another way of saying slave labour. It's a secret code for put on a sissy apron and cut up vegetables in the cafe kitchen, set the tables, fill the salt and pepper shakers, fold the table napkins—and not so they look like baby nappies. It means check the iced water supply in the fridge, wipe any finger marks off the glass counter top, and make sure there's soap, clean towels and paper in the customer toilets. And check for spiders who might think the customer toilets are a nice place to live.

Show time means that at the end of the night, when I think everything is done, there'll be something like a lasagne tray to scrub out, and I hate that because there's always a bit of gloop that won't scrub off in a hurry. It makes me exhausted just writing about all the jobs I have to do. I think Mum tries to sneak in something extra for me every time they change the menu. But when I tried telling her that, she talked about responsibility and working as a team, so that the cafe will be somewhere people like to visit.

She also said, You know we couldn't do without you, Ari.

Sometimes, though, when I'm outside doing my practice and I hear Mum calling "Show time!", I really don't feel like going inside. I want to keep playing and playing until it's too dark to see my fingers on the violin strings. Not playing scales or the exercises Mr Lee sets me to learn each week. Sorry, Opa, sometimes not even the things you've written out for me.

It's the music in my head, there as easily as a daydream.

Sometimes it happens when I hear a song on the radio or on a CD, and all of a sudden there's a whole accompaniment the violin can play.

Mum says: Ari, you should be writing these ideas down.

Jamie says: Ari, the way you do that is the way I cook sometimes, adding interesting ingredients to a basic recipe. You were playing music that way when I first met you at the markets.

It happened like that yesterday, before the cafe opened.

Someone—Mum or Jamie, Allison or maybe even Ben—put a CD on while they were setting up in the kitchen. And one of the songs reminded me of water and waves. It reminded me of the ferry ride from Brindisi to Corfu, when Mum and I went on our first big holiday. It was an overnight ferry trip, and at dawn she took me out to the deck to watch the sunrise and hear the sound of the water under us.

And suddenly, I had a tune for the violin. When I played it out, I liked the sound of it a lot. Which was why I didn't feel like going inside to set tables or check the customer toilets for spiders.

Mum called a few times and then came outside to get a bit bossy with me.

But when she heard what I was playing she still said, That's really nice, Ari. What is it?

I don't know, I answered like always, I made it up.

I can hear her calling right now. She thinks I'm still outside somewhere and she's calling, "Ari! Show time!" But I'm here at the computer.

So it's show time, Opa, and I have to go. Love Ari.

CORFU

aged 6

The shower was the size of a small cupboard and
Mama had to stand at the open doorway to shampoo
the salt and sand out of my hair.

The room she had rented for the week was
shared with two girls from Norway. The old lady who
owned the house lived upstairs. When she first saw me,
she ruffled my hair and said something in Greek,
which made me look to Mama for a translation.

"Schön," Mama said. *Beautiful*, I think. Lucky Ari!

I pulled a disgusted face, worried that maybe the
old lady thought I was a girl. Despite that, I liked her
smile, with its missing teeth, and the fact that she
offered me handfuls of little chocolates from a big
glass jar when she thought Mama wasn't looking.
Though when Mama found out, she made me share
them with her.

We climbed the winding dirt path to the old church that sat above the town and the sea. In the courtyard outside was a priest with a grey beard and black robe, who hand-rolled a cigarette but hid it from view when the tourists got their cameras out. Inside, the church was small and dark. There were religious pictures decorated with gold paint and a sweet smell of incense. The sea below the church and the cliff was the blue of the sky.

When we walked out of the town along a different track, we found a tiny beach, no bigger than my room at Opa's, to call our own for that day and the next. Mama smeared cream over my face and shoulders to stop the sunburn and I waded knee-deep into the rippling waves.

At the end of each day, we washed in the cupboard-shower and walked to the centre of town for food. In Kérkira, it was never dark until well after my usual bedtime and, the later at night it became, the more people seemed to be out and about: walking, sitting or eating.

At the cafe in the town square, there was a mother with a boy about my age, and when we heard them speaking German, it seemed we had someone to have a conversation with. At first, Mama thought that Sandra was travelling alone with her child as well, but no.

My husband runs a computer company, Sandra told us. We go somewhere different each year for holidays. He's back at our hotel—she paused and tapped her head—sleeping off all the wine he drank last night.

The boy's name was Florian and I tried making friends with him. Behind us were kids playing a chasing game around the town square.

"Kann ich spielen gehen?" I asked Mama. *Can I go and play?*

Near where I can see you, she told me.

Come on, let's play! I said to Florian, but he huddled down into his chair and shook his head, first at me and then at his mother when she tried to persuade him.

I went anyway and it didn't matter that I couldn't understand a word of the Greek being shouted around me. The rules of the game were no different to what I was used to at home, and I spent quite some time darting from tree to lamppost to table, dodging adults, dogs and the kid who was chasing us. Gradually, the other children were called away by their parents, and I went back to where Mama sat with Sandra and her boy Florian.

Florian was complaining. He wanted a hamburger and a coke for dinner, not dolmades or bureks or anything Greek. He was bossy and spoke more rudely to his mother than I would ever dare speak to mine. And when his father suddenly appeared beside our table, he sounded much the same. Florian's father wore split-lens glasses and looked like a doctor. He greeted Mama and I with a smile, but then frowned when he spoke to his wife. They were supposed to be meeting friends for dinner, why wasn't she back at the hotel getting ready?

She smiled an apology at us. Sorry, I have to go. It was nice meeting you. See you again before you travel on, perhaps.

And so Mama and I sat alone once more, surrounded by Greek voices and laughter. After we had eaten, she ordered more drinks for us: wine for herself and fruit juice for me. And I watched her face settle into a faraway gaze. After a couple of wines, I knew that one of two things usually happened—Mama either got funny and loud, telling jokes and singing songs. Or she got quiet and sad, remembering and missing my father. I rested my chin on my hands and watched her.

She saw me staring. Are you tired yet, Ari?

"Noch nicht," I told her. *Not yet.* After a day of walking and swimming I was really, but felt happy to sit in the crowded cafe surrounded by other people's noise and laughter. When I looked back at Mama after a moment, she was wiping her eyes with the back of her hand, and I was out of my chair immediately.

"Was ist los?" I asked. *What's the matter?*

She sat me on her lap, swallowed the last mouthful of wine. I'm okay. I was thinking of Sandra, her husband and his computer company, and how clever your own dad was with computers. And I'm sitting here making decisions about things—like going back to university and finishing my degree, and exactly where you're going to spend the rest of your childhood.

"Ich verstehe das nicht," I told her. *I don't understand.*

We leave for Amsterdam the day after tomorrow and soon the holiday money will be nearly gone. Everything I've saved from a year of part-time jobs. And maybe we won't travel again for a year or two, because I want to keep the part-time work going somehow and save for an even bigger journey and holiday next time.

She looked at me for a little while, as if expecting me to respond. When I didn't, she added: Next time we travel, Ari, we'll go by plane.

Where will we go? I wanted to ask, but there was a burst of noise from the back of the cafe and cheers from the people around us. In a corner near the cafe kitchen, three musicians and a singer had crowded themselves onto a tiny stage. A song began, and the music jumped and danced around the words. I'd never heard music quite like this, but enjoyed it straight away, and felt Mama's body relax behind me. I went back to my own chair, she ordered another drink each for us, and suddenly she was smiling.

Ari—food, drink, people—music!

So I knew that for the time being, things would be okay again, and forgot to worry and wonder about what she'd said.

Your bedtime was about five hours ago, she told me when finally we stood up to leave. Which is why you're nearly asleep on your feet.

She knelt down. On you get. A piggyback ride home for my tired, well-travelled boy.

And we set off across the town square, still crowded and noisy.

Don't you fall asleep just yet, Mama said. You're usually quite easy to carry, but if you're asleep, it's like a sack of potatoes on my back.

And to keep me awake, she sang cheerfully through the midnight crowds and all the way to the house with the cupboard-shower.

LEAVING

aged 8

Such a long way, Opa said to Mama. The other side of the world this time. Such a big trip for a small boy.

I could see his face in the rear-view mirror, looking at me more than I was looking at him. There were lots of new and different places to look at outside the car, and it was such a long drive it already felt like we were far away from home.

Call me, Opa said. Reverse the charges, don't go wasting your holiday money. Call me and let me know how you both are.

Stop worrying, Mama smiled, putting a hand on his shoulder. We'll be fine, we have so many contacts.

She held up a piece of paper that had been in her tote bag, which I'd seen already a few times—names, addresses, phone numbers, all given to her by friends and relatives who had travelled before.

Australia, Opa said. Further than I've ever been in my life. Just let me hear from you, okay? A postcard or a letter won't be enough.

He was looking in the rear-view mirror again.

Christmas somewhere different, he said. And two months without school.

Mama put her address paper back into her bag, replying, And you know how quickly he'll catch up when he returns. Anyway, his teacher gave him a few things to work on while we're away.

Opa smiled at her. As a matter of fact, so have I.

Mama rolled her eyes and said, I can't begin to guess.

At the airport there was a bigger and different violin case in the boot. It looked like one of Opa's special concert violins but, when he opened the case, I saw it was a Cremona Stradivarius copy that he'd found at the markets in Göttingen before Easter.

But it's three hundred years old! Mama protested. It's valuable!

It's a copy, Opa told her, shaking his head. Then to me he added, but it's a good copy. I think you're ready for a three-quarter size. It plays beautifully and you'll enjoy getting to know it.

Mama rolled her eyes again and sighed loudly.

In your backpack, Opa told me, you'll find a new workbook of music that I've put together for you.

Whenever we talk on the phone, see if you can play me some music, too.

After waiting patiently as we lined up for baggage checks and boarding passes, he said to us, Have a wonderful adventure. Bring back lots of interesting stories and beautiful photos, won't you?

He hugged and kissed Mama, then swept me up in his arms, and held me so tightly I thought he'd never let me walk through the glass doors to the departure lounge.

Ari, was all he managed to say. Ari.

SYDNEY

aged 8

Emil.

I must have looked startled when my father's name was mentioned, because Mama noticed straight away.

"Du bist gewachsen," she explained. *Piet just said you've grown so much since they last saw you. And that you have your father's face.*

It felt odd hearing about him so far from home, and I couldn't think of a way to reply, standing among the noise and crowds at the airport.

In the old house a few streets from the beach, Piet said it again: Emil. He looks so like Emil.

Mama looked pleased; she nodded and smiled.

I thought I remembered Piet and Ellie, and their kids Tali and Jochen, from long ago, but couldn't be sure. I recognised Piet and Ellie from photos in my mother's albums. She and my dad first met them while travelling in Europe.

Was I there? I asked, and Mama nodded, patting her tummy.

This is where you were. Turning cartwheels and practising your soccer kicks. And Jochen was doing much the same in his mum's tummy. You boys have nearly the same birthday.

Because Tali and Jochen had already lived here for two years, their talk jumped from Dutch to English and back again. At first, we got by with pointing and hand signals, but after four or five days, I was beginning to find my way through the puzzle of unfamiliar words for simple things.

"Was sagt sie über mich?" I had to keep asking Mama. *What are they saying?*

In the heat of an afternoon, Jochen and I sprawled ourselves across the sofa and floor cushions to watch videos, while the ceiling fan beat above us like helicopter blades. Above the talk and noise on the TV screen, I suddenly heard Mama's voice from the backyard, my name mentioned, and then lots of laughter from her and Ellie.

"Was ist los?" I asked her when I went to find out why. *What is it?*

They were sitting in the shade near the back steps. Nothing, Mama fibbed. We're talking about the joys of travelling with children.

I pulled a face. "Mamaaa," I said, feeling a bit cross and embarrassed, wondering which story about me had made them laugh so much.

Tali was out in the backyard as well, with two of her friends from high school. "Mama!" one of the friends squeaked, and the three of them began giggling and whispering.

"Girls," Ellie scolded them, "you're not being very nice."

"Was sagt sie über mich?" I wanted to know. *What are they saying?*

"Sie findet dich richtig süss," Mama said in my ear. *They think you are very cute, saying "Mama" like a talking doll.*

"Yuk," I said, not wanting to be cute at all.

"Sorry, Ari," the girls chorused.

"Actually," Mama added quietly, "I think you're cute as well. Especially when you're asleep."

"Muuum," I groaned out loud and, before I'd realised it, the word had escaped. It sounded like Tali and Jochen when they complained to their own mother about something like bedtime.

My mother smiled and ruffled my hair. "How is the movie you're watching?" she asked me in English.

"It's good," I replied. "It's funny."

"When it's finished, we go to the park. You can get some music practice in before dinner time. Okay?"

"Okay," I answered, and added "*Mum*", looking over at Tali and her friends, daring them to giggle some more. They didn't.

"You don't need to go all the way to the park," Ellie told Mum. "We haven't heard Ari play for ourselves yet. We wouldn't mind the sound of a violin for a little while each day, you know." She and Piet kept insisting, until finally Mum said to me, "Come on, my boy—out to the backyard," and sat with me while I practised my scales and the pieces Opa had put into my violin primer. In a corner of the lounge room was a guitar that belonged to Piet or Ellie; Mum borrowed it to play alongside me on some songs we often did together at home.

Everyone left us alone to practise, but came outside when they thought we'd finished.

"Wow," Ellie said to me. "So it wasn't just your mum boasting. Ari, you play very well."

"You both do," Piet added.

"Not me," said Mum. "I don't play much music these days—I'm out of practice."

"Your mother," Piet said to me, "is way too modest. She plays very well and she has a wonderful voice. You two should do some busking while you're here, you know. You've been to the Saturday markets down near the beach; there's always people playing music there. You can make yourselves some money.

Ari, tell your mother to stop shaking her head at me—"

I packed the violin away and went back inside to play computer games with Jochen. Even though I heard Mum say several more times how out of practice she was with her playing and singing, she hardly had the guitar out of her hands for the rest of the night. Even as I lay awake in the guest room, I could hear the adults' conversations around the barbecue in the backyard, and then the sound of music and my mum's voice, as she sang and played songs I hadn't heard in a long time.

"What do you think, Ari?" she asked me the following afternoon as we sat in the park beside the beach. She'd listened quietly as I'd played my scales and exercises, but looked at me now, waiting for an answer. I didn't realise what she was asking about at first.

She had brought the guitar with her, and took it out of its case to strum as she spoke. "About playing at the markets," she explained. "Not putting on a big show or anything. Just finding our own quiet little spot, sitting down and making music. Like now."

I shrugged, not ready to say yes or no.

"I know lots of songs," Mum told me. "Last night I realised how many I remember, so I don't mind doing most of the work. And you've played for an audience before—the relatives at home, the kids in your class at school. It would be a different way for you to practise your music. Whenever we've been here in the park, someone always stops to listen. If we play some music at the markets and don't really enjoy ourselves all that much, then it doesn't matter. At least we've given it a try."

I shrugged again.

"Say something, Ari!"

"You should be talking to me in English," I replied. "Piet said we can make lots of money."

Mum laughed. "So are we doing it for the money or the music?"

But my attention was elsewhere. I could hear the thud of waves on the beach and the sounds of traffic and sirens on the roads behind the park.

Emil, Piet had said. *He looks so like Emil.*

"Mr Daydreamer," Mum sighed, and played the guitar some more. The notes chimed like a bedtime song, and I copied them onto the violin, fingerpicking the strings at first, then letting the bow take the tune somewhere quite different. I liked the sound of us playing together, and I tried to make the music last until I could work out a way of finishing the tune properly, to drop my notes to a sleepy whisper.

"And what tune was that?" Mum asked.

I blinked my eyes and stared at her a moment, as though I'd woken from a nap. "I don't know, I made it up."

Which she must have known. "And if I asked you now the notes you began with, could you tell me?"

"Yes. G, F, E flat, D, C ..." I recited it like a jumbled alphabet.

"You have to write these tunes down, Ari, these tunes you make up. They're too special to lose; they're like photos." She paused and reached over to pat my shoulder. "It's very special the way you compose music—special to me and Opa, maybe special one day to lots of other people." She held her hand still on my shoulder.

"You should be talking to me in English," I said again. "You said I had to practise."

"And you'll be getting a smacked bottom if you keep being cheeky," she replied, which made me laugh. I couldn't remember ever being smacked.

"I still haven't heard an answer about playing at the Saturday markets," she said then. "Yes or no, Ari?"

"Yes," I said at last. Not only because we'd just managed a nice tune together, but because it had reminded me we were a long way from Hattorf, a long way from Opa's house. I had a sudden picture in my head of Mum playing music by herself at the Saturday markets, and it was a picture I didn't like. She and I were a long way from home, and I decided we needed each other. Because, the way I saw it, there was no one else.

Saturday markets

aged 8

I am eight years old.

Ari. A–R–I.

I have played violin since I am, I *was*, three years old.

Yes, really. My Opa, my grandfather, taught me. But I teach myself now as well.

Thank you.

"You're improvising!" he said. I remembered his face from the Saturday before, when he'd stopped longer than other people to watch and listen to Mum and me playing. I recognised him as one of the group of musicians who played at the other end of the markets, the busy part where the cafe and food stalls were. He played drums and other instruments that you hit or rattled. "You're improvising," he said again, then turned to Mum and asked, "That wasn't something in his music book, was it?"

"Mama," I said, "was hat er gesagt?" *What did he say?*

"He does this by himself," Mum told the stranger. Then to me she explained, He says you are improvising. It means making music up as you go. But in the right key, in a way that shows you know what you're doing.

"Oh," I nodded, and knelt down to flick through *Mein Drittes Geigenbuch*, My Third Violin Book.

By our third Saturday at the markets, people stopped all the time to talk to Mum and sometimes to me.

How old are you?

What's your name?

How long have you played violin?

Who taught you to play like that?

The first Saturday, we had chosen this quiet end of the markets, just a few clothing stalls, a fortune teller and not many people. And when Mum started playing Piet's guitar, it was so soft you could hardly hear it, and her singing voice was as quiet as though she were talking to herself.

But then Piet, Ellie and their kids turned up to become our audience for a while. They clapped and cheered, had a bit of a laugh and a joke with us. It made things a little different, made Mum's voice louder and happier. After that, more people stopped to watch and listen, to throw coins into the open guitar case. We took it in turns, Mum and I—sometimes just her singing, sometimes just me playing, usually the both of us making music together.

"Just till lunchtime," she said. "A morning is quite enough. In the afternoon we can spend our music money on holiday things—a movie, a ferry ride, the zoo ..." Which I liked the sound of.

I had chosen one of Opa's little jazz pieces to play next but, when I stood up ready to begin, the stranger—the drummer—was still there.

"You've played some interesting songs," he said to Mum. "Not the usual stuff people with guitars play at markets. And your voice is great. Have you done much of this before?"

"Not here," Mum told him, "not in this kind of place. At university in Germany, I did a lot of theatre and music. A long time ago." She pointed at me. "When he was a little baby."

"You're Illona and Ari, aren't you?" I looked more closely at him when he said that; saw blond hair cut to a short fuzz, small tinted glasses a bit like the ones Opa wore.

"We are," Mum replied, and raised an eyebrow as if to say, How do you know?

"I'm Jamie. I know Piet and Ellie. My bunch of fellow musicians are taking a bit of a coffee break. Which could well become a lunch break and then a beer break. Can I bring my instruments and join you here for a bit? Play some music with you?"

"Yes, why not?" Mum replied. "What do you think, Ari? Someone else to join us for a bit?"

"Es ist mir egal." *I don't mind.*

"And what has happened to the English you should be practising?" she asked me.

When Jamie returned, he carried a snare drum, a pair of brush sticks and a shaker. I put the violin down and sat to listen to the sound of him and Mum playing music together, unsure at first about the idea of this extra person—though I liked the way his drumming kicked the songs along a little, and I thought I could hear Mum's voice differently as well.

"Ari," Jamie said eventually, "you were choosing something to play earlier. Want to try it out now?"

I thought about that for a moment, then nodded. Opa had written out a little jazz piece called "Serenade For A Cuckoo", something I had practised lots and that Mum and I had tried together in the park on several afternoons. So although *Mein Drittes Geigenbuch* was open at the right page, I barely needed to glance at Opa's notes by now. Positioning my fingers and arching the violin bow, I began the melody alone.

With a sideways glance, I saw Mum and Jamie each tapping the beat out, and then heard both of them begin to play their own instruments at exactly the same moment.

Without meaning to, I found that I was enjoying myself. At the end of eight bars, there was the *t-tsh-click* of the brush sticks and snare, then Jamie saying softly, "Again!" After sixteen bars, he murmured "Guitar solo!", which made Mum giggle a bit. By the time we had played the tune right through several times, a big crowd had gathered, and they clapped loudly once we'd finished. Lots of coins clattered into the open guitar case, and someone in the crowd shouted, "More!"

"Thank you both," Jamie told us, shaking each of our hands and smiling a wide smile. "Will you be here next Saturday? Mind if I join you again?"

"What about your other musicians?" Mum asked.

"It's a very casual arrangement. Sometimes five turn up, sometimes ten. It's fun—but you two are something different. May I?"

So, from then on, whenever we played at the markets Jamie would turn up as well to play for half an hour, maybe an hour with us. And he always brought a different selection of instruments.

"Percussion," he told us. "My favourite thing."

"What's it called?" I had to ask each time, and over a couple of Saturdays learned vibraphone, bodran, maracas, marimba and temple blocks.

Sometimes we'd see Jamie during the week, and wind up in one of the cafes near the beach, where he and Mum usually did most of the talking. He found out all about us and the other times we'd travelled. We found out that he wasn't only an occasional musician, but also worked as a chef in a hotel bistro.

"I worked full time as a musician once, a long time ago," he told Mum. "I used to be married, too, used to run my own restaurant. Come to the bistro one day and I'll do lunch for you."

Soon our holiday had another pattern to it; a pattern where Jamie fitted into our days. "When do you have to go back?" he asked one time, and he actually looked sad as Mum told him, "Two more weeks."

"Really?"

"I have to. It's been holiday time for kids here, but not where we live. Ari has actually missed quite a bit of school while we've been away. He's clever with his work, but he needs to return. And my father is expecting us home. So ..."

"Will you come back here? More travelling, another holiday?"

Mum nodded. "If I have the money saved. Next time I'd like to buy a cheap car and do some proper exploring. See more rainforests, more beaches, a bit of desert."

"But when?" Jamie asked, and Mum could only shrug in reply.

"Well," he said after a moment, "then you must come to dinner, both of you. My place—I'll cook. It's only a short walk from Piet and Ellie's. Okay?"

I thought that Jamie would need a big house to fit all his musical instruments into and, on a Friday night, when Mum and I walked to the address he had given us, it was an old warehouse in a back street—nothing to look at from the outside, but like a museum on the inside.

"Welcome," Jamie said at the door. "It's not elegant, but it's cheap and a short walk to the beach."

Inside there was just one big room that was the size of a church, with a high, high ceiling and not much furniture. Just a table and chairs, a sofa, a bookshelf and a bed tucked against a far corner. But there were lots of musical instruments, the ones that Jamie brought to the markets and many others besides—a guitar or two, a big drum kit, bells on a frame ... and a piano.

"A baby grand!" Mum said in a surprised voice.

"Divorce settlement," Jamie said, pulling a face. "My ex got the sports car, I got the piano."

"Don't be touching anything," Mum told me.

"No, it's fine,' Jamie said. "Ari is a musician, too. Have a bit of an explore, and touch or play whatever instrument you like."

So I did, wandering and poking about, rattling things, picking notes out on the baby grand, flicking through a couple of music books that I found on a small table. When I looked back to Mum and Jamie, it was because their voices had gone from normal talk to quiet things I couldn't quite hear. It felt a bit strange.

But then I found the best thing of all. On the floor beside the bookshelf was a xylophone made completely out of glass, each piece set carefully on a glass frame.

"Mama, schau dir das an!" I called out, interrupting their quiet talk. *Look at this*! "Es ist wunderschön." *It's beautiful.*

"If you can say it in English," I heard Mum reply, "then you should. That's better manners."

I sighed to myself. "Come and look," I called back, and she came to see.

"I made it last winter," Jamie told me. "Have a go of it, Ari, and see what you think."

I picked up the mallets that lay beside the glass xylophone and tapped a few keys to make a tune. The sound echoed softly around me, as though I was hearing it played underwater.

"Es ist wunderschön," I said again, to myself this time. Mum and Jamie watched and listened to my music-making for a while longer, before walking back to the sofa and their quiet talk.

Jamie's food at the bistro was nice, but the food he cooked in his home was even better.

"I'm just an employee at the bistro," he said as we ate, "but one day—one day—it'd be nice to get into the restaurant business again. I don't know where or when ..."

He had rented a couple of videos for me to watch after dinner, so I settled myself and my full tummy onto the sofa, and stayed there a long time. Whenever I glanced away from the TV screen, Mum and Jamie were still sitting with their empty plates and full wine glasses, still talking and, finally, holding hands across the table.

Will we come back? I wanted to know on the walk home. Will we stay with Piet and Ellie and the kids next time? Is it true you'll buy a car and we'll go exploring the outback? Will we see Jamie next time? What were you talking about with him?

Till Mum stopped on the footpath out the front of Piet and Ellie's and said, "Ari! Zu viele Fragen!" *Too many questions!* in a voice that wasn't quite scolding but came close.

I am eight years old.

Ari. A–R–I.

I have played violin since I was three years old.

Yes, really. My grandfather taught me. But I teach myself now as well.

After several weeks of Saturday markets, I was used to people watching me play, and even used to having my photo taken sometimes. But on the final Saturday, during the Bach piece that was for violin only, I caught sight of a different kind of camera.

When I finished, as people clapped and threw coins into the open violin case, I saw the TV station sticker on the side of the movie camera the guy in the baseball cap was pointing in my direction. As he clicked it off and held it down by his waist, a girl with a clipboard stepped forward and introduced herself to us.

"We've had a few calls," she said, "about the great music that's happening down here. And the fact that one of the musicians is extremely young." She smiled at me when she said that last bit. "We've just filmed and interviewed the jazz blues group that play up near the cafe. Can we interview you and do some more filming?"

"Only if it makes us very rich and famous," Jamie replied.

"For a TV program?" Mum asked.

"A human interest story," the girl with the clipboard replied. "Something different for the close of tomorrow night's news bulletin."

"Das ist mir peinlich," I told Mum. *I'm embarrassed.*

That made her laugh. "You should be excited," she said.

It felt strange seeing myself on film the following night.

I had already sent an e-mail on Piet and Ellie's computer: Opa, I think I'm going to be on TV. They filmed me playing music at the markets. We're going to record it and bring it home with us to show you. See you next Friday. Love Ari.

Of course, the girl with the clipboard had wanted me to play a nursery rhyme, but I wanted to play some Vivaldi instead. It should have been note-perfect, but it wasn't quite because the TV camera had made me a bit nervous. The second thing I played felt better because it was Opa's little jazz piece that Mum and Jamie joined in with as well.

"Talented things come in small packages at the esplanade markets," I heard the clipboard girl's voice say. I wanted to disappear under Piet and Ellie's sofa, but was surrounded by the entire household. Mum, Piet, Ellie and their kids had crowded around the TV for the Sunday evening news. Jamie had taken some time off from the bistro to watch it with us, too.

"You're not embarrassed still?" Mum asked, hugging me. "Don't be. Everyone is very proud of you."

The camera came in close to my face as I played my Vivaldi.

"Ich mag Vivaldi am liebsten," I said from the TV. I had refused to speak English for the camera.

Then Mum was there as well, translating for me. "He likes Vivaldi best of all," she said. Which wasn't completely true.

The music on the TV changed to our jazz piece and the screen showed me, Mum and Jamie, and the faces in the crowd smiling at us. Then the clipboard girl's voice again, saying, "Ari Huber and his family have been entertaining the crowds down here for most of the summer break. But it all came to an end this Saturday, as they fly out of Sydney next week."

I saw my face again as the news credits rolled across the screen. I could see how hard I concentrated on my music, that my eyes watched every movement of my fingers and the bow.

Everyone in the lounge room clapped and began talking at once.

I let out a big sigh, grinned and felt a bit pleased

with myself. I knew that Opa would be happy when he saw it.

Family, the girl with the clipboard had said. Ari Huber and his family.

When she said it, I'd glanced sideways at Mum, but she and Jamie were already looking at each other.

ON THE STAIRS

aged 8

I had my Wild Things slippers on. They were furry grey with three claws on each foot, just like the monster feet in the *Wild Things* picture book I'd had since I was very little. Except the slippers didn't really fit so well any more, and my toes were bunched up at the ends like fingers in a fist.

Time to give them up, my mother kept telling me. You've had them since you were five, and you're eight and a half now. Time to pass them on to cousin Björn. He'd love them.

She was back at university again and I was back at school in Hattorf. I could tell she wasn't so keen on university any more, and I knew there was something else she was unhappy about.

I found out what it was the night she and Opa sat talking in the kitchen. It was late and their voices had kept me awake, so in my too-small Wild Things slippers and my too-big blue pyjamas, I sat on the stairs between my bedroom and Opa's kitchen to listen.

Mum's voice: I feel like something major has happened. That if I don't pick up on it, it'll be lost forever.

Opa's voice: So why hold back? Emil would have wanted you to have a happy life.

When my father's name was mentioned, I began to understand that they were talking about Jamie. He'd sent us postcards and letters, e-mails on Opa's computer, and had phoned up every once in a while. It was funny to hear his voice on the phone, sounding as close as if he was in his warehouse and we were still only a short walk away at Piet and Ellie's.

"Hey Ari," he would say in my ear, "how's life? How's music?"

"Opa's teaching me Stephane Grappelli," I'd tell him, knowing that Mum would be standing nearby, ready to grab the phone and take it outside, where she would talk for ages in the quiet voice she'd used at Jamie's house.

In the kitchen, I heard Opa say: I told you this was home for you and Ari for as long as you wanted. But it shouldn't be forever and you shouldn't feel bad if it's time to move on. You've a whole life still ahead of you, and so has Ari.

Mum's voice: But I'd be taking him so far away. From his friends, from the family. And from you.

Opa's voice: And the world is a much smaller place these days. A conversation by phone or computer. A day and night by air. We'd miss each other, but we wouldn't be lost to each other.

On the stairs, I was getting colder and colder. I rearranged my legs and hands, curled myself up to hang onto the last of the warmth from my bed. It was no good, and my loud sneeze gave me away well and truly.

And then Mum was at the bottom of the stairs, calling out, You should be asleep, you've got school in the morning!

But I was already most of the way back into bed, kicking the Wild Things slippers across my room and doing a terrible job of pretending I'd never crept out from under the covers.

You should already be asleep, she told me crossly from the doorway.

When I peeked over the quilt, I could see the shadowed shape of her baggy jumper and her mop of dreadlocked hair. She had her arms folded and I heard a long sniff; it was as though she was crying, or had been. Finally her face was next to mine, and I got my second bedtime kiss for the night.

Sleep, she instructed. I don't want to see or hear from you until morning.

We're going back, aren't we? I said.

She stood up straight again and didn't say anything at first. Yes, she said at last. Yes, we are.

BYRON BAY

aged 9

I was lost.

In the time it took to be distracted by the lady fire-eater and the man juggling tennis rackets, I'd lost sight of Mum and Jamie.

Just after Christmas, we'd driven a long way up the coast to Byron Bay. Mum had heard a lot about it from other backpackers and wanted to see it herself. Not just for the ocean and the beach, but for the hills and rainforests a short distance away. Summer holidays meant crowds of people, the smells of sunscreen, food, incense and salty air. It meant traffic jams and noise.

"New Year's Eve in the Bay is a lot of fun," Jamie told us. "Lots of partying and music. But I know a quieter place where we can stay and escape to when we feel like it."

He drove us to a camping ground beside an

inland river, where we pitched his silver and green dome tent.

I'd never camped in a tent before, and had to get used to sand grit everywhere and to the smell of mosquito coils. Mum hated the thought of itching insect bites. We slept on a huge air mattress, between sheets that smelled of Jamie's car—petrol, rubber and dust. We stayed up late, talking with people from nearby tents and caravans, and woke up early enough to see the sun rising over the river.

During the day, we almost lived at the beach. I liked the sun and heat, the push and swirl of the waves, but was afraid when my feet couldn't touch the sand under the water. When Jamie realised I didn't know how to swim he started to teach me, holding me afloat while I swung my arms and kicked, pushing me towards the shore if a bodysurfing wave rose up behind us.

I thought I knew the town well enough by now, but it was New Year's Eve, night-time, and suddenly everything looked quite different. There were so many people, it was hard to find gaps in the crowd where I could look for Mum's sunflower-patterned top or Jamie's purple T-shirt. In the dark, it was difficult even to tell colours properly, though the streetlights were on and the cafes and shops all lit up. But at my height, I was in shadow and hidden from Mum and Jamie's view.

I'm lost, I'm lost. I could feel fright and panic rising in my throat and mouth, a moment I'd felt once or twice before in crowds at airports and other unknown places where we'd travelled. Even with better English now, the moment of panic began to stretch into minutes.

I thought of calling out, but I also wanted everything just to turn out right without attracting too much attention. I wasn't sure whether to stand still or begin walking.

There were hundreds of people in the main street of the Bay having their New Year's Eve parties. A rock band played on the back of a truck trailer, their music thumping through speakers the size of house doors. People were shouting, dancing, wobbling everywhere, and I was bumped into and trodden on. When I began to walk in the direction I'd last seen Mum and Jamie, my feet and soft sandals nearly found a broken beer bottle. Too soon, I was at the end of the shops and cafes, the edge of where everyone was.

I walked back towards the middle of the crowd, back to where the fire-eater and the tennis racket juggler were, and I was trying hard—very hard—not to start crying like some little kid. The panic and fright wouldn't go away, but just when I was really starting to get scared—I was found.

"Ari!" Jamie pressed a hand onto my shoulder.

He looked wide-eyed and relieved. "Found you! Thank goodness!"

"I was walking, just walking," I said quickly and breathlessly. "I looked away and then I couldn't see you."

"Your mum is in a total panic. She takes you through ten countries, a couple of continents, halfway around the world—doesn't lose you once—and loses you here!"

"Sorry."

"Hey, it's nobody's fault. Just gave us a bit of a fright, that's all."

"Where's Mum?"

"Searching the next block. We're meeting up outside the pub. Our next stop would have been the police station, otherwise."

"Sorry." This time when I said it, my voice was shaky.

"Hey," Jamie said, kneeling down beside me, "don't get upset. You're okay, that's the main thing." And he gave me a quick hug, something he'd not done before. "Now, we need to find your mum. So you can be on lookout duty."

"How?"

"Up here." And as though I weighed next to nothing, he lifted me up onto his shoulders and began walking back through the crowd. I could smell cigarettes, beer and food, things that either made me breathe in deeply or my nose twitch. Heads and faces bobbed all around, and every now and then I'd see another boy or girl riding on an adult's shoulders.

It was a long time since I'd been carried by anybody. I was too big and heavy for Opa now. Mum used to piggyback me sometimes on our walks through distant towns and forests, but would now only scoop me up for a hug and a goodnight kiss.

And I thought of my father. He used to carry you everywhere in that baby backpack, Mum said when she had given me the photo in the silver frame to keep on my bedside table at Opa's farm. I thought about that photo now, about little me in a nappy and warm clothes, somewhere colder and far away, riding on my father's shoulders. I wanted to remember when that photo had been taken, but couldn't.

Jamie's hair wasn't crinkly like my father's had been. When I looked down at Jamie's head, his hair was light and polished away on top to shiny skin. I had a good view now of his bald patch, of the freckles on his head like a map of stars. He smelled of salt air and the beach.

I spotted Mum where Jamie said she would be.

"Wo warst du?" she demanded, looking twice as relieved as Jamie had, but sounding cranky as well. *Where were you?* And she spoke crossly at me in German, loud enough to make the people around us turn to see what was happening.

I tried to explain it the way I had to Jamie, but it didn't calm her down straight away.

All the times we've travelled, she said, and you should know what to do when lost in a crowd.

"I think he got quite a scare, Illona," Jamie said, putting a hand on her shoulder. "Don't let it spoil the night. He's safe, that's the main thing."

Mum nodded, but rolled her eyes as well. "I know. I've just aged ten years in ten minutes, that's all."

"Half an hour till midnight," Jamie said then. "Supper on the beach? The sound of the ocean as the New Year begins?" He looked at Mum, then added, "And …?"

She nodded a quick reply, as though something else had been planned as well. Jamie set off in search of food while Mum, as though reminding me of how I'd worried her by getting lost, took me by the hand. We walked to the beach end of the main street and sat in the park, where the grass gave way to sand.

There were people here, too, having late-night picnics and parties. On the beach was a giant sand sculpture that someone had modelled during the afternoon. It was a dragon, stretched out like a cat, looking out to the ocean. Little candles burned brightly under the folds of its wings.

I could hear the waves hissing across the sand.

"I'm sorry about before," Mum said. "It was the dark and the crowd ..." I heard her take a deep breath. "Ari, I've got something to tell you."

"What is it?"

Suddenly, unexpectedly, she was nervous, and what she had to say came out in a big rush.

"Married?" I finally repeated, and my own voice had gone as croaky as hers.

She nodded. "Maybe you guessed a little already. It's something I'm ready for, and it means a great deal more than I can explain right now. But I have to know that you're happy about it too."

"Is Jamie coming back to Germany with us?"

Mum took another deep breath. "No. We're coming here." And she took my hand again with both of hers, held it up to her lips. "We won't be tourists any more. I've found somewhere I really like being, and someone I really like being with. Jamie has music, laughter, the friendship I need ... Ari, are you angry at me?"

I shook my head, but in a sudden panic had a rush of questions. What about school and my friends, what about our family? What about Opa?

"That," she said quietly, "will take time to get used to. For me as well. It means our holidays in future are trips back to Germany. And probably only once a year, if that."

"But what about Opa?" I asked again, knowing that if I kept saying his name, I'd be in tears.

"He knows already. I've talked it over with him so many times, even more than you've overheard. And he wants it for us, too. He's encouraged me to make this decision. He's happy and he's also a bit sad. He's going to miss you very much. And he wants to talk with you about it. So when we call him tomorrow ..." She wrapped her arms around me, let me lean back against her chest. "Ari, you're shivering," she said, resting her chin gently on my head. "What are you thinking?"

And I shrugged, because I couldn't explain panic, sadness and the way things change. I managed to say, "I like Jamie, and I like it here. I like it here, but I miss Opa."

"I know, Ari."

"Will I have to call him Dad?"

"Who, Jamie?"

"Yes."

"No, I think Jamie is quite happy to be just that—Jamie. He cares a lot about you, you know that."

"He's funny," I said, then added for no particular reason, "When I teach him things in German, he makes it sound all tangled and wobbly when he tries to speak it himself."

"You're right, he does."

I could hear the music and party noise in the main street behind us and the voices of people nearby in the park and on the beach. I stared at the sand dragon, then wriggled further into my mum's hugging arms. And we sat for a while, watching the ocean and listening to the waves.

Jamie returned with a large cardboard tray of food and drinks.

"Ten, nine, eight—" The crowd in the main street was shouting a New Year countdown, "—three, two, one!" There was an explosion of cheering and the pop, crackle and colour of fireworks in the sky.

"Happy New Year," Mum said, kissing me on the head, and kissing Jamie on the lips when he leaned over.

"Frohes Neues Jahr," he said to us.

I think he meant the same thing, but the way he pronounced it made us laugh.

FROM A PAYPHONE

aged 9

Opa, we're moving. We're leaving the city, moving up to the mountains. Jamie found an ad in the newspaper, and on the weekend we all went for a look.

It was a really long drive; three hours in the car to get there. And it's a cafe, on the road to some tourist caves. It has two really old fuel pumps out the front that don't work. And an old sign on the roof that says "Mayfair Cafe".

We're going to turn it into a cafe again, Opa. It hasn't been open for years, but Jamie used to run a restaurant in Melbourne when he was married before. So he knows a lot about food and cooking, and the stuff he cooks us always tastes really nice. And Mum's an okay cook, too.

Opa, she's punching me on the shoulder, and she says to tell you she's a wonderful cook. Even when it's buttered toast, it's to die for. So it should be a cafe people like coming to. It's going to be vegetarian, because that's all Mum and Jamie eat. Though they let me have hamburgers and things like that every now and then.

We borrowed the keys to the cafe so we could look inside and explore. There were old lemonade and ice-cream signs, a big glass counter, and an espresso machine that Jamie thinks he can get repaired. And this cafe, it's a bit weird because it's got a stage. Up the back, with lights, velvet curtains and everything. Jamie and Mum were talking about having music as well as food.

We can live there, too, because there's a house out the back. You walk through the cafe kitchen and along this hallway nearly all built out of old windows. And at the end, there's a whole house. Two bedrooms, a lounge room, a bathroom, another kitchen and a verandah. There's an old garden and then nothing else but trees and bush.

It took us fifteen minutes to drive back into town from our cafe. It's too far for me to walk or ride a bike, so I'll have to catch a bus to get to school. We had lunch in town and tried to think up new names for our cafe. Jamie was making jokes about vegetarian food and wanted to call it the Lentil Nightmare or Cafe Fartypants. We all laughed, but

Mum said she had something more elegant and refined in mind.

And in the cafe, Opa, I counted twelve tables, and forty-four chairs all painted blue. And guess what? Chair number forty-five is painted yellow. It's really strange. Mum and Jamie were talking about repainting all the chairs, but I told them the chairs were fine the way they are. And not to paint the yellow chair so it matches the others. I don't know why, I just like it that way and—

I was out of breath and almost out of news, and paused long enough to realise how quiet it was at the other end of the phone.

Opa?

I'm still here, Ari. It all sounds really wonderful. And your yellow chair, maybe it should be something special for the person who sits there. When I worked with the orchestra, we often had rehearsals at a particular studio. One of the chairs in the rehearsal room had a wonky leg; it was very annoying to sit on. The person who got the wonky chair usually did a bit of cursing and swearing, and had to find bits of cardboard to make the chair sit evenly. The rest of us would usually laugh about it. But we made a rule—if you sat on the wonky chair, then you had to buy the violin section a drink after rehearsal. Over a year, nearly everyone had a turn. So my thought is—something for the cafe customer who sits on the yellow chair, but not something unkind. You'd like your customers to come back, after all.

A free coffee?

Fast food places do that. This is not going to be hamburgers and chips, it sounds a whole lot better. So something special; a free dessert maybe. You know what, Ari?

What?

For a free dessert, I'd come all the way to Australia. All the way to your cafe.

When will you visit?

There was another silence at the other end of the phone, then a reply: I don't know, Ari.

And I wasn't quite sure what to say next.

THE MAYFAIR CAFE

aged 9

Hi Opa, guess what? Mum got all her hair cut off. That's right, no more dreadlocks. She drove in to pick me up after school, and when I got into the car I nearly screamed. She looks funny, like she's back at school herself. Her hair is so short, and she put this crimson colour in it.

That was on Monday. By Wednesday, I was sort of used to her new look. She says it's for the cafe, that she wants to look elegant. Not just for serving food, but for singing songs as well.

Tomorrow night is our opening night.

Mum and Jamie have been rehearsing for the past month. They invited their friends out and tried different menus on them. Piet and Ellie came all the way from Sydney to stay one weekend. It was fun playing with Tali and Jochen again.

After the food, Mum and Jamie tried out some of their music. Jamie had his baby grand piano sent up from the city and now it's on the stage in the cafe. A girl from the uni is going to play it, and Jamie's going to play the drums and percussion. Allison, the girl is called.

On the second weekend of food and music practice, a guy on a motorbike turned up. He'd seen the ad for a kitchen hand that Jamie put on the noticeboard at the uni in town. Then another guy arrived, this time in a ute. There was a mattress on the tray in the back, and it looked liked somebody was tied to the mattress. Except it was a musical instrument.

The guy with the motorbike said his name was Ben, and that he had kitchen experience and played double bass—and could we use him?

I told Mum I wanted a Celtic tattoo on my arm, like the one Ben has. But Mum said, Not very likely, my boy!

The music sounded good—a bit different from what Mum and Jamie first played together at the markets, though. Their friends ate all the food, and drank lots of wine, and made heaps of noise clapping, as if Mum, Jamie, Allison and Ben were big stars.

I watched everything from the arrival lounge. That's this big old sofa, sort of velvet like the stage curtain. It was in the house, but we carried it out to the cafe and put it near the fireplace. That way, if customers arrive tomorrow night and all the tables are full, they can wait on the arrival lounge.

I told Mum she looked like a movie star. Next to the bookshop where she works part time there's a secondhand shop, and she bought a few of these dresses with straps and frills. She looks really different when she wears them; you might not recognise her at all if you come to stay. When are you coming to stay?

This bigger kid at my school, Gareth Yardham, told me that if our cafe was going to do nothing but vegetarian food, then it must be crap, that we must be hippies—that Mum probably has hairy armpits and boobs down to her knees. He said it three times, so I hit him. He told on me and I had to miss lunchtime play. Mr Carthy, the principal, said he was surprised at me.

We're going to do the idea you had about the yellow chair. It's going to be my job to move it from table to table every Friday and Saturday before we open, so that it's always a surprise for a lucky customer.

But that's only one of my jobs. Mum and Jamie have worked out a whole list of things I have to help out with in the cafe. Like setting the tables and clearing away dirty plates, which is what I had to practise the nights when Mum and Jamie's friends came out to test the food and music. Luckily, Jamie bought a new dishwasher for the cafe kitchen, because I sure hate washing and wiping up. I tried to get out of doing jobs by saying I had violin practice. But that's at four o'clock and my cafe jobs start at five o'clock.

I'm halfway through the sixth violin primer, Opa. The Berlioz piece is *really* tricky. I'll play it to you over the phone next week.

I miss you, too.

FRIDAY ASSEMBLY

"Ari," Samantha Aliberti said to me at school one day. "Ari. That's a pretty cool name, you know."

We were doing maths experiments with some other kids in the class. Whenever we did maths activities, I always tried to be in the same group as Samantha because she was good at her work and she didn't waste time. And she stood up to other kids when she knew something wasn't fair or right. "Must have been dead easy learning to write your name when you were a little kid."

"It was," I agreed.

"You should try learning how to write 'Samantha'! It took me ages to get all the letters in the right order. And the right way around."

"I knew how to write my name when I was two."

"Why, because it was easy? Or because you were a genius?"

"Oh, both." I meant it to be funny and that was the way Samantha took it.

"So can you still speak any German?"

"Only a bit," I fibbed.

"Okay, say something."

"Like what?"

She shrugged. "About school."

The other kids in our group had stopped their work to listen, so I couldn't really clam up and refuse. I took a breath and said, "Dieses Rechnen ist zu einfach."

"What does that mean?" several kids all asked at once.

"This maths," I told them, "is too easy."

I had never said anything at school about music and the violin. In kindergarten in Hattorf, it had been fun for show-and-tell. But here at this school, it would have felt like showing off.

"No it wouldn't," my best friend Thomas tried telling me. "The kids in our class would get a real surprise."

It didn't make me change my mind. Our school had a band that lots of kids were in, and when Mum had read about it in a school newsletter, she wanted me to join.

"Mum, it's not that kind of band," I said. "It's not like an orchestra and it's not music like you play in the cafe. The school band does pop tunes and marching stuff, the national anthem. The violin wouldn't fit in."

Samantha was one of the kids who was in the band, honking away on a saxophone when they practised during lunch breaks. The kids in the school band were all different ages and from nearly every class in the school, so I could understand how tricky it was to get everybody playing more or less the same tune. It was something Opa had once told me about the orchestra he'd played with: Even adults, Ari, can be a nightmare when it comes to rehearsing a piece of music.

Sometimes I couldn't help finding the school band funny to listen to—there was always, *always* someone out of time or out of tune. And Mrs O'Hearn, the Year Four teacher who organised the practice sessions and conducted the band whenever they played for the rest of the school, got pretty carried away with her conducting. She pulled funny faces and her hair went haywire.

At school assembly one Friday, the band played a new piece they'd learned. It gave me the giggles.

Thomas was sitting next to me and he got the giggles as well. In fact, he got the giggles so badly that he fell sideways off his chair and onto the asphalt. Mr Carthy glared at us, then sent us out of assembly and over to wait outside his office.

Thomas and I could still hear the band tooting away as we leaned against the wall beside Mr Carthy's office door.

"That sounds so funny," I said, "like cartoon music."

And Thomas, who always had to go one better, said, "I nearly wet my pants!" That gave us the giggles all over again—just as Mr Carthy walked in.

"Is something still funny?" he asked crossly. "You two weren't just letting your class down, you were letting your school down. I think you can miss your playtime, the pair of you. Go and get your lunches, then take yourselves to the time-out seat and sit quietly. I'll speak to you again later."

The time-out seat was right outside Mr Carthy's window.

"Will he ring our parents?" I asked Thomas.

Thomas shook his head. "Don't think so. You get a note home if you're sent to the detention room, and a phone call for a parent interview after three detentions." Thomas was an expert on all of this.

The window behind us slid open. "You're not out there for a conversation," came Mr Carthy's voice. "Move away from each other and sit quietly."

So we did, silently fidgeting while the rest of the school had their lunchtime play. We'd gotten over our giggles by now.

The sun was warm on my face, and I closed my eyes. I hoped Samantha Aliberti didn't think I'd been laughing at her saxophone playing, because she'd actually sounded pretty good the times I'd heard her practising alone.

Ari. That's a pretty cool name, you know.

Somewhere, sometime, I had asked Mum about my name. I asked because I knew she had been named after a great-aunt, that my cousin Björn had been named after a famous tennis player. That another cousin was called Vashti because her parents had travelled to India and met a child with that name. So when I asked Mum, she told it a bit like a fairy tale, the story of Ari Cormier, the boy I was named after.

Well, once upon a time ... she began, and told me about a little kid who, ages and ages ago, had lived in New York; who had spoken French and English; whose mother had been a model and a singer, and had known an artist called Andy Warhol.

Somewhere, Mum said, I've a CD of Ari Cormier's mum singing. She was German and had quite a rich, deep voice. Before you were born, I found photos of her in a book, and then one of her son as well. You even looked quite like him when you were little. I just liked the look and sound of his name, and it stayed in my mind until you were born. So you were called Ari, after a boy who led an interesting life.

What happened to him? I asked.

I don't really know.

And his mother what happened to her?

She became ... Sometimes Mum couldn't find the words she needed in English, and would click her fingers in the air, searching.

Famous? I suggested.

No, the opposite.

Unpopular?

No ... Obscure, that's it. Obscure. Only performing and recording occasionally. Living in different places. She died in Spain, a long time ago now. One time I went with friends to visit her grave in Berlin, in Grunewald-Forest.

Was I there?

Oh yes. Rugged up and asleep in your stroller.

I thought I remembered it, but wasn't sure, because there was also a picture in my head of the cemetery in the town where my father was born. In the yard of the church where he had once sung in the children's choir was a stone that said: Emil Huber 26 Jahre. I remembered tracing over that writing with my finger and collecting flowers and little stones to make a pattern on the ground beside my mother as she sat and stared into the distance.

Later, much later, in the weeks when we had first

come by plane to stay at Piet and Ellie's house, Mum tapped me on the shoulder and said, There he is.

Who?

We were outside a music store on a Sydney street.

The other Ari. The one I named you after.

We were in the way and people were stepping around us. In the window was a display of poster photos all the same—four musicians with their instruments, a girl on a stool with her hand resting on a microphone and, walking past them all, a blond-haired boy much younger than me. It was as though he was in the photographer's way and shouldn't really have been in the photo at all.

Four CD box set, I read in English. What does the rest say?

An anniversary edition, Mum explained. They were a very influential group of musicians—even your Opa likes their work and they weren't exactly what you'd call classical. The girl on the stool is Ari's mother. And there's Ari, your namesake.

We did look alike, he and I.

Even now, I sometimes thought about the other Ari. About whether he married or went travelling, whether he became a musician, like his mother. Whether he was still alive.

I wondered how I would look to him, in trouble

at school for giggling during a school assembly. Or at the cafe, wearing a white kitchen apron and standing at the sink, washing salad greens. Maybe the other Ari would be more impressed if he knew that I was a musician, and that—

"Ari Huber, you're looking almost too comfortable there." It was Mr Carthy, speaking just before the end-of-playtime bell rang. Thomas was already standing up; he and I traded uh-oh looks.

"I'm not very impressed," Mr Carthy told us. "That probably should have been a detention."

"Yes, Mr Carthy," Thomas and I answered together.

"Can you explain to me what was going on?"

"I started it," I said. "I got the giggles and couldn't stop."

"It was me most of all," Thomas said.

I knew that when I owned up to being in trouble at school, Mum would probably sigh and say, That Thomas. He's a nice kid and I know he's your friend—but you and he together are not always a good combination. Ms Orton must be the most patient teacher in the universe.

I didn't get into trouble at school quite as much as Thomas did, but I wasn't about to let him take the blame for being sent out of Friday assembly. So I said, "It was me that started it. One of the kids in the band, someone on a trombone, was half a tone out. It made the music sound a bit, well, strange."

Mr Carthy looked at me. "Ari, you're not in the school band and, as far as I know, you're not a musician. Yet you're telling me that you and Thomas were disrupting assembly and falling off chairs because a trombone was half a tone out?"

Then Thomas dobbed me in. "Mr Carthy, Ari *is* a musician. He's been a violin player nearly all his life. I heard him play to his grandfather on the phone last year and he's really, really good. So maybe he knows about tones and stuff."

I looked darkly at Thomas. He shrugged back at me.

Mr Carthy sighed and said, "Go and join your class, both of you. Any more silly, disruptive behaviour at school assemblies, and you'll be in the detention room faster than you can say 'trombone'."

"Yes, Mr Carthy," Thomas and I answered in our most serious voices.

"And Ari ..."

"Yes, Mr Carthy?"

"When our school forms its string quartet, your name is first on my list."

SLEEPOVER

last August

"How come," Thomas whispered, "how come your mum is singing with her eyes closed?"

We were both on the arrival lounge and whispering conversations to each other as Mum and Jamie rehearsed some of the evening's music. "It's like she's falling asleep because the music is boring."

"It's a love song," I whispered back. "It's supposed to sound, you know, romantic."

"Urk, kissy kissy *lurrve* stuff."

"So maybe it wouldn't sound romantic if she was staring like a zombie at the audience."

"An audience of two. Us."

"It doesn't matter. She still has to get it sounding right." This made Thomas think quietly for at least a minute or so.

"Still looks a bit weird," he said finally.

I suddenly remembered. "I said the same thing, once."

"What?"

"About Mum singing with her eyes shut. When I was really little. She was back at uni for a while and did lots of theatre and music. I was about three or four years old and in the audience with my grandfather. Mum and a bunch of musicians were on stage doing a song. And I said in a really loud voice, 'Why is my mum falling asleep?' People in the audience started laughing and then the people on stage did too. Mum had to stop singing because she was laughing as well. After everyone had clapped and cheered a bit, Mum tried doing the song a second time, but she kept her eyes open."

"And you remember that?"

"Mum reminds me about it sometimes."

"Well," Thomas said, "I can remember falling out of a tree when I was four, and breaking my arm. Then I fell off my bike when I was six—I bashed my head and there was blood everywhere. And I got into trouble on my first day of school."

"Your first day?" I shouldn't have been surprised.

"We were singing 'I'm A Little Teapot' with Miss McDonald. And I was doing armpit farts to the music."

For the first time, Thomas had come to spend the weekend. I had worried that it might be boring for him, because I thought I'd still have to help out in the cafe. "I usually show people to their tables," I told him, "and that's after I do the vegetable cutting and stuff like that in the kitchen. And I clear plates and load the dishwasher."

But when I mentioned it to Mum, she said, "I think we can give you the night off. Thomas will be your guest, so keep him company."

"And keep him occupied," added Jamie.

I had already spent a couple of weekends at Thomas's place in town. His parents had let us dial out for home delivered pizzas. We'd gone rollerskating at the rink near the train station. And Thomas's big brother Eric had chosen us a couple of horror-movie videos and we'd been allowed to stay up late watching them. How could I match pizzas, rollerskating and horror movies?

Thomas's parents had dropped off his bike, so that was something we could both do. We rode up to the pine forest and I tried to describe the one near my grandfather's farm.

"We can ride to the lookout next," I suggested, but Thomas shook his head. Back at home, we played soccer until it was too dark to see the ball properly. We sat on the arrival lounge while Mum and Jamie rehearsed. When Allison and Ben turned up for work, I introduced them to Thomas. It felt strange watching them do the evening preparations without me.

I remembered that Thomas liked fantasy stories and was always drawing maps of imaginary places, so I got Jamie's big atlas out of the lounge room bookcase and showed Thomas all the real places I'd ever been: Hattorf, Corfu, Amsterdam, Byron Bay … I found my old passport in my treasure box of badges and school merit awards, and let him laugh at the photo of me, aged six. Then it was my turn to laugh at him trying to read the German print.

By now I could hear the faint noise of customers in the cafe, their voices drifting along the hallway into the house. "When you two are ready and hungry enough," Mum had said, "come up to the kitchen. Tell Thomas he can order anything he'd like from the menu." So we did; it was something I was always allowed to do for myself on cafe nights.

Afterwards, I thought Thomas would want to go back to the house and play a computer game or watch a video but, no, he wanted to be in the cafe to see the musical part of the evening.

We sat ourselves on the arrival lounge again with our desserts, watching the cafe customers and listening to the first few songs. I kept glancing sideways at Thomas, expecting him to be fidgeting and restless.

But he sat more quietly than I'd ever seen him do at school.

Only after a long while did he whisper, "Back in a minute," and then he walked off towards the hallway to the house. Pee break, I would have guessed, except he was back almost straight away, talking more loudly against the music of a noisy song.

"Ari, the phone in the house is ringing."

It was weird, the sound of our phone in the empty lounge room, away from the crowd and noise of the cafe. And the sudden, familiar sound of my grandfather's voice through the handset: Ari! How are you? How is everything?

"Hi Opa!" If I sounded surprised, he didn't mention it. Everything is fine. I've a friend from school here, Thomas. He's spending the weekend. It's a cafe night here—you don't usually call us on cafe nights.

I knew it would be, he replied. So where is your mother at the moment?

"Auf der Bühne." *On stage.* Main course is over and the music is on. Do you want to speak to her?

No. But I'd be happy to hear her singing. Can you take the phone close to where she is?

Thomas was making silly faces and pointing at the phone. "Is it long distance?" he whispered. "Is that your grandad?"

I nodded. "Back in a minute," I told Thomas, and carried the handset up the hallway, stopping beside the glass counter in the cafe. Where I stood with the phone was shadowed and dark. On the stage, Mum, Jamie, Allison and Ben looked pale and ghostly under a blue spotlight. Even though the tune was cool jazz, the sort that normally would have made me click my fingers or tap a foot, I stood completely still, hugging the handset to my chest until the song finished and the cafe was noisy with clapping and cheers.

"Opa, wie fandest du das?" *What did you think of that?* I was almost back in the lounge room again, but he hadn't replied. Are you still there?

Oh yes. That sounded wonderful. She sings so well, your mother. Ari, I'd like to hear from you now. What can you play me this week?

Play? Now? "Go back out to the cafe, if you like," I said to Thomas, who'd settled himself into Jamie's reading chair. "I have to stay on the phone a bit longer."

"That's okay," Thomas replied. "I don't mind. It's interesting hearing you speak another language."

It wasn't quite the answer I wanted. "I have to go get something," I said, giving Thomas the phone. "Here, you can say hi to my grandfather while I'm gone."

"Me? What will I say? I can count to ten in Danish, but I can't speak German."

"It's okay. Opa understands most English." I could see Thomas wasn't very sure about this. "Go on," I encouraged him. "Just say hello and talk about soccer or something. He'll understand you."

"What are you doing?"

"I have to get something from my room. He wants to hear me play."

"Hear you play what?" Thomas asked as I passed him the handset.

In my room, I got my violin out, quickly checked the tuning and found a page in the latest primer Opa had sent.

I could hear Thomas's voice: "Hi, I'm Ari's friend Thomas." Pause. "We're in the same class at school." Pause. "We did heaps of bike riding today and played soccer, too. My legs are still sore." Pause. "Ari's a really good player. When we're at school and he's goalie, it's really tough getting the ball past him." Pause. "Yes. Here's Ari back again, Mr … um—he's got a violin with him." Turning to me, Thomas asked, "What are you going to do?"

"Play some music. I play a bit of music to my grandfather nearly every time he phones up."

"Play some music? I didn't know you did that."

"Well, I do." I was expecting Thomas to say

something smart and humorous. "Hold the phone up close to the violin," I said, then leaned over near the handset to say to Opa, "Beethoven, Egmont Overture excerpt."

Even with my eyes focused on music, strings and bow, I could see the look on Thomas's face, wide-eyed and surprised. He still had that look after the minute or two it took me to play Opa the little piece of Beethoven. That, and the bit I added on.

I took the handset back from Thomas. Did it sound any good, Opa?

Very good, quite accurate. Some more practice and it should sound wonderful. And what was that bit at the end? Not Mr Beethoven.

"Ich habe das erfunden." *I made it up.*

I thought as much. Something else you should write down and make something of in the future.

There was another gap of silence, then Opa added, You're a wonderful and very promising musician, Ari. A wonderful grandson as well.

It wasn't the way I was used to Opa speaking. "Willst du mit Mama sprechen?" *Do you want to speak to Mum?* I didn't quite know what else to say.

No, no. Tell her I called and I'll speak with her soon. And regards to Jamie. Tell your friend Thomas it was nice to speak with him. And there's a new book of music heading your way soon. In the meantime, practise that Beethoven! Bye Ari.

"Tschüss, Opa." I said it a second time, just to be sure. *Bye*. But the dial tone was sounding in my ear. I put the handset back into its cradle beside the kitchen doorway. And realised Thomas was still staring.

"What?" I asked. "What is it?" And I laughed a bit; he looked so surprised.

"What you just did," he answered. "That music you played. I didn't know you could do that. *How* did you do that?"

I shrugged. "It's just something that ... I do. I've played violin ever since I was little. My grandfather taught me."

"But you sounded like a grown-up," Thomas said. "Don't put the violin away yet! I want to hear you play some more."

"Get out of it, Thomas." I pulled a face at him.

"No, really. Play something else."

"No way. And since when did you like violins?"

"Since I found out five minutes ago that you can play one."

I tucked the violin under my chin and played five or six of the most disgusting noises I could manage. Once Thomas had his fingers plugged in his ears and was making gurgling noises, I took the violin to my room and packed it away. "Don't tell anyone at school I can play," I told him.

"Why not?"

"Because I don't want the other kids thinking I'm ..."

"Weird?"

"Something like that."

"Well, I don't. I think it's a bit, you know, amazing." He paused and added, "Your grandad sounded like a nice guy. My grandad's a real old grouch."

"Yeah?" I couldn't imagine Opa as a grouch. "It was strange, though," I said. "Opa never usually calls on a cafe night."

"Maybe he wanted to surprise you," Thomas said.

"Maybe." And I thought about it some more. I couldn't remember the last time Opa had heard Mum sing.

RAIN

last September

Your hair is wet, Mum told me. Your face is wet, your clothes look soaked through—

I felt like riding my bike.

What were you thinking, going away like that?

I just felt like it.

You know I don't like you being here at the lookout by yourself. And she knelt beside the log seat I was on, close enough for her umbrella to stop the rain showering on my face. I glanced up for a moment, long enough to see the umbrella's crazy pattern of sunshine clouds and bright blue; the real view from the lookout was misting rain and low fog that hid the deepest parts of the valley from sight.

You didn't even put your bike helmet on, she said.

How did you know where I was?

I didn't need to be a detective to follow bike tyre tracks along muddy ground. Anyway, Jamie came out after you and saw which way you were riding. As soon as he heard your music practice stop as suddenly as it did. As soon as we heard the door slamming.

I don't want to play the violin ever again.

Hey. She said it quietly and gently, wrapping a hand around my shoulder. I was sure it would make her own jacket wet, squeezing like that against my soaked sweater. Hey.

We shouldn't have left him by himself, I said.

Who, Jamie?

No! Opa! I hadn't quite meant to shout it like that.

But Mum just sighed and answered patiently, We talked every week on the phone. Your aunts were calling by at the farm every couple of days. Your cousins often dropped in after school or at weekends. Opa might have lived by himself, but he wasn't alone.

We shouldn't have left him.

But we did, Mum said. And it was the biggest, most difficult decision I've ever had to make. I needed to start my life all over. I don't expect you to understand that just now, but that's how it was. It wasn't easy for me then. And it's not so easy at the moment.

She was quiet for a minute or two, then said, Opa was eighty-four, Ari. That's not a bad age to reach. He worked hard, he had a good life and there were more than a few rewards along the way. I was his surprise daughter; he wasn't expecting to be a father again at fifty. And you were the surprise grandchild. Just when your Opa thought there'd be no one to pass violin music on to—she paused, as though catching her breath—there you were, asking to be taught.

I didn't want to look at her, or to believe that anything in the past three days had really happened. I made myself gaze at the view from the lookout.

Mum tightened her hug and kissed me on the head. You're shivering, so we need to get ourselves home. You can walk your bike back with me, then get changed into dry clothes. Jamie's probably worried enough by now to come looking for us if we stay here any longer. Come on.

I hadn't realised how cold I was until I felt Mum's warm hand take mine.

PLAYTIME

last September

It felt like I'd been away a long time.

"I don't feel like going to school," I had told Mum over breakfast.

"You know," she had replied, "I don't really feel like opening the cafe again on Friday night, either. I don't feel much like singing to an audience, never mind the cooking and waitressing. But we both have to try. It'll be hard for us at first. But maybe it's better than doing nothing and feeling miserable."

So I went to school, and two weeks away felt like forever.

The playground was a rush of noise and voices.

Hi Ari! Hey Ari, you're back. Did you go overseas or something? Thomas said you went to a funeral.

But they hardly waited for me to answer Yes to

everything before racing off to get in some playtime before morning class began. Everything at school was suddenly loud and fast, but I could only feel tired and quiet and slow. I wasn't even sure what I wanted to do, so I sat on one of the seats near where some little kids were playing. And I stared into space and kept very still.

"Ari!" It was Thomas. "Hey, you're back. Didn't know when I'd see you again." And he sat himself down beside me, waiting for me to say something, to start a conversation.

When I didn't, he added, "I was wondering when you'd come back. Want to go and play soccer?"

But I shook my head. I could see the kids from our class down on the flat grass near the back fence, the best place for a proper soccer game. I could see the view over the fence as well—the town, the deep valleys and hazy mountains.

"Handball?" Thomas asked.

But I shook my head again and it made Thomas go quiet. I could feel him looking sideways at me and then, unexpectedly, his arm was around me, resting on my shoulder. It was the sort of thing little kids might do when they're with their best friend. But it wasn't something that I thought Thomas would do, because if the other kids in our class saw him, we'd both be teased.

"I'm sorry about your grandfather," he told me. "He sounded like a nice man when I talked to him on the telephone that time." Thomas lifted his arm away and waited for me to say something. When I didn't, he added, "I've never, I mean, no one in my family has ever died. Not that I can ever remember, if you know what I mean. So I'm sorry, Ari."

I wanted to stand up and go get my schoolbag. I wanted to walk the fifteen kilometres home, but I knew I couldn't. I wanted to say: I don't want to talk about it.

Except of course I did. So I nodded my head, looked at Thomas, and tried to say something.

An e-mail, Monday night

Opa, we had snow.

The kids at school told me when we first moved here that it snowed sometimes in winter, but I didn't believe them. I have to now! Because when we woke up today, there were drifts of white in the cafe garden and out the front beside the road. Not enough to get me a day off school though, because the bus still came for me. But the road was icy and the driver had to go more slowly than usual.

Mum and Jamie and me went for a walk up to the pine forest this afternoon. Whenever I ride my bike, it takes me ten minutes to get there. But it took us more than half an hour walking, because we stopped to have a few snow fights along the way. So it was just about dark by the time we got home again. The pine forest is just like the one near Hattorf, all shady and still and mysterious. I like it.

I'm supposed to be doing my homework now, a project to hand in to Ms Orton by Friday. I chose rainforests, because we drove north to one in the last school holidays. It was shady and still and mysterious, too. I've done my project heading and a border of vines and tree roots. But the whole middle bit is empty because I haven't typed out any information yet. Ms Orton takes marks off if you hand things in late, so I have to get typing soon. But I'll type to you first.

We're getting heaps of customers at the cafe. When it first opened, Mum and Jamie weren't sure if it was going to work out, but then a lot of students from the uni started turning up for meals. And then families from town—sometime kids from my school come in with their parents. Everyone says they like the food, and if they stay for the music they like that, too.

Jamie's music and Mum's voice always sound great. Sometimes the songs are really quiet, sometimes they're noisy and sometimes they're funny.

Other people play music here as well. Some uni students turned up last Saturday with electric guitars, so we had rock and roll half the night. Some of the customers danced, then Mum and Jamie had a bit of a dance as well. I sat on the arrival lounge and laughed.

Another time, some older people turned up; they'd been bushwalking all day. After they'd eaten, they asked if they could have a go on the piano and some of the percussion instruments. They played some really neat jazz. It gave us a surprise.

Someone did a review of our cafe in a city newspaper. We didn't even know about it till Allison rang to tell us. "Anything but average," the review said, and awarded us three and a half stars out of five. Mum and Jamie drove into town for a bottle of champagne to celebrate with.

The cafe is cool fun, Opa. It's like having different, interesting people visiting our house two nights a week. I never get bored.

There are still drifts of white snow in the garden and it's freezing cold outside. I know because I just went out to check. But it's almost my bedtime now and I haven't typed anything for my project. And I can hear Mum coming to check up on how I'm going.

Bye Opa. From Ari.

CHRISTMAS PAST

last December

When I was a boy, Opa had told me more than once, it often snowed in Hattorf at Christmas. And something has happened to the climate since then. Cold and grey at Christmas, yes. But snow, never quite. It arrives later, in January.

I wanted it to be snowing when we arrived in Hattorf for Christmas. Plenty of things had changed at Opa's farmhouse, but not the winter weather.

Monika and Tim, my aunt and uncle, lived here now. It was their car parked at the garden gate, and mostly their furniture inside the house. Occasionally there was something I remembered that had been my grandfather's—a framed picture, a reading chair, the long table in the kitchen. What used to be the guest room now belonged to my cousin Anya, while the upstairs room that had once been mine was now

Björn's well and truly, filled with his bed, his soccer and music posters, his books, toys and computer games.

It was noisy when we first arrived, a chance for my relatives to meet Jamie properly at last, and to say to me, Du bist gewachsen, Ari. *You've grown.*

But I didn't say much back straight away, and explored the house I had once lived in quietly and a bit sadly. When I got to the door of Opa's study and opened it a little, it was the one room that hadn't been changed. I could see at a glance that all of Opa's things were where I'd always remembered them being. I clicked the door shut again quickly and went back downstairs.

In the morning, Björn was awake first. I could hear his voice somewhere downstairs, along with the TV. The spare bed was where my own used to be, but everything else in the room was quite different. Even the morning sounds from downstairs were different. Opa had never allowed the TV to go on in the morning. Putting a CD on was the first thing he had done each day.

On Christmas Eve, all the other aunts and uncles and cousins arrived, and the house was filled with more luggage and spare bedding, more conversations that usually began with, Du bist gewachsen, Ari, and apologies to Jamie if too much German was being spoken.

Some of my cousins were shy at first but then Tabea, who had just turned eleven, wanted to know some Australian swearwords. Suddenly I was able to laugh and joke around. We went outside to play and explore, while the adults sat around the kitchen table. They drank wine, and talked and laughed more loudly as the afternoon turned into evening.

They were musical, my relatives, and left their conversations at one point to sing. They had brought guitars, an accordion, an electric keyboard. My cousin Anya, fourteen now, brought out the silver flute I'd heard her learning since she was nine—breathy, unclear notes then, but piercing and accurate now. Someone found a big book of carols and folk songs that had belonged to my grandmother. It was set on the table and everyone began to work their way through songs I either knew well or soon remembered.

Uncle Karsten was the noisiest of the adults and he had a terrible singing voice. Ari, he said, we need a bit of violin here. Go up to the study and bring one of Opa's down.

Everyone was looking at me. I shrugged a reply, unable to answer either yes or no, and took myself out of the kitchen and up the stairs.

In the past three days, I hadn't set foot in the study, but now I made myself open the door and go to Opa's desk. If it had been daytime, the view out of the window would have been the back garden and the field that finished at the pine forest.

The study was a very full little room, with rows and rows of novels, art books, music folios, encyclopedias and the sheet music Opa had collected all his life. There were orchestra and concert portraits on the walls, music stands, and spare bows in an open box. And arranged along one wall beside the desk were the violins in their cases, all four of them—from the tiny one-eighth I had first learned on, to the very special concert Schuster. I looked at each of them in turn, then gently, carefully got the Schuster out and held it under my chin. But it felt big and fragile, like something that didn't quite fit me. I put it back into its case, and knew I wouldn't be able to play any music tonight. Then I heard Uncle Karsten's voice from downstairs—"Ari, Ari!"—and then the kids all joining in too. It sounded like a soccer chant.

There were footsteps on the stairs and Mum stood briefly in the doorway. She went down again, and I heard her say, in English, "Hey Karsten, cool it." Jamie's voice asked a question then, and Mum said, "No, it's okay. I'll go and talk with him." Then she was beside me where I sat at Opa's desk, one hand on my shoulder, a wine glass in the other.

"You okay?" she asked, and when I shrugged, she said, "Hop up. Let your weary mother have a seat." She set her wine glass on the desk and gently sat me on her lap. "You're not too grown-up for a hug, my boy."

"Everything's different," I said softly. "Except in here."

Mum nodded. "Sometimes things have to change. And it's hard, but it's the way of the world."

"I don't want to go downstairs and play music."

"It's okay, everybody understands that. Even Uncle Karsten, who's had rather more red wine than everybody else." She swept a hand slowly around the room, then looked at me. "Ari, you'll be able to choose whatever books or sheet music you're interested in from this room. Your Opa left it in writing."

"I don't want anything."

"Well, as one of the musicians in the family, it was his wish that you become the keeper of some of the things he treasured. That includes the instruments as well."

"I said, I don't want anything."

"Okay. It's something to think about, though."

We sat for a while, listening to the sounds of conversation and music downstairs.

"It's nearly Christmas," Mum said then, "and we should be down there with everybody, not up here by ourselves. Everyone was so looking forward to seeing you again. Björn has been driving his parents crazy for the past month—When is Ari coming? How many days till Ari gets here?"

"Has he?"

"So you should be spending time with him and your other cousins. Monika and Tim have been talking about coming to visit us next Christmas. But that's another year away. In the meantime," she squeezed me with another hug, "it's time for us to be downstairs. Come on."

On the way out, I turned the study light off, but this time I left the door open.

I must have fallen asleep at the table, because I woke up in the dark on the guest bed in Björn's room, my shoes off but the rest of my clothes still on. I could hear my cousin's sleep-breathing nearby, and the soft voices of adults downstairs.

The room was lit from outside, a near-to-full moon shining bright and blue against the shadows.

It's Christmas Day now, I guessed.

And for the moments I was awake, I imagined that outside the window there were little flakes of snow swirling in the moonlight, the way Opa said Christmas used to be.

THE PACKAGE

Two boxes arrived at the post office in town.

When we went to collect them, it took the three of us—me, Mum and Jamie—to carry them out to the car. They were addressed to Mum, plastered with German postage stamps, and they weighed a ton.

"This has cost them an absolute fortune to send," Mum said. "Monika and Karola, my mad sisters. What have they sent me?"

Remnants of your misspent youth, Aunty Monika had written on a note inside the first box. The farmhouse needed tidying. Now that your home is down-under, we thought you should have some of your special things. We enjoyed sorting through them! Hope you do too.

"A Pandora's box," Mum remarked. "Just what I need. Or maybe don't."

Opening and unpacking the first box was a bit

like an early Christmas, though the things inside made Mum pull all sorts of faces. There was a high school photo album that had her horrified and embarrassed by the sight of old boyfriends, old hairstyles, the things she used to wear. There were postcards from past holidays and the places she took me; a soccer team scarf, a doll, some books. Some things she looked at fondly—my christening photos, a pair of my baby shoes, a picture from my first day at school, holding the cardboard cone of sweets my teacher had given to me and the other kindergarten children. And there was a big collection of CDs. By the time the first box was unpacked, our lounge room floor was covered with all these sorts of things.

Inside the second box was a second letter.

"Ich bin dran mit schreiben," Aunty Karola had scribbled. *My turn to write.* This box is for Ari. There's something special that belonged to his father and to his father's father before. We hope that Ari is not too grown-up for it and that he enjoys being the new custodian.

It was a tiny electric train set.

Jamie, who'd been busy making funny remarks about the family photos Mum had been sent, about how white everybody's legs were in the beach holiday snaps, became all serious and interested as I unpacked the little boxes.

"Oh wow, I used to have a train set when I was a kid," he said, as he sat cross-legged on the carpet beside me, "but this is a real quality one. Look at all the detail in these carriages; there's even tiny passengers on the seats. Amazing! Will it work on local electricity? Do we need an adaptor? Can we have a go at setting it up?"

I knew how special it was and felt excited about it too, but in a quieter way than Jamie, who was turning into a big kid before my eyes. I'd never known about the train set and wondered where at Opa's house it had been kept. Jamie and I took it all out to the empty cafe and started setting it up on the floor near the stage. When we'd finished, it was a mini-world—trains and carriages, a maze of straight, curved and branching tracks, tunnels, little railway stations with tiny plastic people on the platforms, houses and buildings. The only thing wrong was the shape of the power plug.

"Easily fixed," Jamie told me. "The German voltage is almost the same as here. With the plugs sorted, it should all work. What d'you think?"

I nodded, enthusiastic.

"You're very lucky," Jamie said after a pause. "This is very special and probably very valuable." Then he added, a little uncomfortably, "Ari, I'm sorry. It would have been extra special if your dad had been able to pass it on to you himself. Instead of me sitting here, babbling away."

"No, it's okay," I told him. Whenever my dad was mentioned, Jamie was always gentle and kind. I felt sorry he didn't have any kids of his own. "If you can fix it so the trains all work," I continued, "that'd be really great. Thanks, Jamie."

The train set made me think a lot more about my father than I let anyone know. Not because of the obvious things, like letters or photos, that had come out of the two boxes. But just something I could feel and, by the end of that week, something I could hear.

Inside the first box had been more CDs than Mum could remember having actually owned. Each afternoon when I came home from school, she'd have one of these discs playing. Some of it was really familiar to me, songs I'd heard and known most of my life.

"Lively up yourself!" she sang loudly at me one afternoon, dancing to a reggae song. She bumped her bottom against mine and nearly knocked me off my feet.

But a couple of times when music was playing, I found her standing very still and listening quietly, her eyes daydreaming.

And then it happened. I was in my room tapping out homework on the computer. One of the CDs had been playing for a while, as Mum and Jamie washed up after dinner and then settled themselves on the couch with mugs of tea and evening talk. The music didn't have words and wasn't really something to dance to, but it wasn't classical either. It sounded more like background music to a movie, shimmering and dreamlike. At first I was only half-listening, but my homework became slower and slower because the music began to sound like something I could play on the violin. One piece finished, another began, and for a moment I sat frozen to my chair.

Then I dashed out to where Mum and Jamie sat. "This isn't one of your CDs," I told Mum. "It's one of—" I paused for breath. "It's one of Dad's."

She looked startled. "Yes, it is," she agreed. "A few of them are. Monika and Karola used to borrow his music from time to time, and they weren't always quick to return things. So some of your father's CDs have turned up after all this time."

I could tell she was about to ask me something, but I said quickly, almost out of breath, "I know this."

"What do you know?"

"This music. This piece of music. I know it, I remember it."

"Ari, from where? No one but your father owned this CD. And it's not something you might hear on the radio every other day."

"I know. But I remember it."

"How?"

"Dad. He used to play it to me."

"Ari, you would have been very little. Two years old, three at the very most."

"When you were at uni," I said, "and he'd look after me at home, in that flat we had in—"

"In Göttingen."

"In Göttingen. He'd play this music and dance me around the room."

Jamie had been listening quietly, and raised his eyebrows thoughtfully. I couldn't read the expression on Mum's face, and wondered if she believed me. "I know this music," I said again. "Every note."

"Did Opa teach you this? He was always finding interesting stuff for you to learn."

I shook my head. "Can I borrow it?"

"Borrow this CD?"

"To play. In my room."

After shutting my bedroom door, I set the disc in the player, found the track and turned the volume down low. And I picked up the photo kept on my bedside table.

The music began, and I traced a finger over the thistle pattern around the frame, staring at my baby reflection. I knew this tune well enough to hum along with it and gazed at the photo until it shimmered like the music. I stared until it moved like a film.

I could see my face, my tiny new teeth smiling, a spray of white-blond hair blowing out from under my woolly cap. The crowd moved around us; I could hear their voices and chanting. The Brandenburg Gate rose up in the background, white stone and archways. I was in the baby backpack behind my father's shoulders and head. His hair felt crinkly in the grasp of my fingers and his jacket smelled sweetly of leather and cologne. Everything in the photo was alive. Everything blurred and focused, over and over.

I pressed the repeat button on my CD player and the music began again. It would be easy to play on the violin, I decided. It had been months since I'd played the violin inside the house, and the volume of it sounded alarming at first. I almost expected Mum or Jamie to appear at the bedroom door asking about the noise. But that didn't happen.

The music played over and over, and so did I. I managed to work out the main theme after only a couple of tries. The minor interludes took a little more time, but finally sounded okay.

The repeat control on my disc player kicked in again and the music began once more. This time, I turned the volume right up so that it more or less matched the violin.

I lost count of how many times I played that music, but I had it note-perfect. At one point, I heard Mum call loudly, "Ari, please, something different!" But I stared across at the photo on the bedside table, played the music through again, and felt a knot in my stomach grow and grow.

Suddenly Mum was in the room. She stepped behind me, gently stopped the bow in mid-draw across the strings, made me set everything down on my desk. Then she turned the volume on my disc player down low.

"Ari," she said very quietly, "Ari, you have to stop now."

And then I started shaking. My face crumpled and I fell into a heap on my bed. Mum sat down beside me and hugged me very tightly. I didn't feel very grown-up at all. I felt like the little baby in the thistle-framed photo.

"You played that really nicely," she told me.

"But how come?" I asked.

"How come what, Ari?"

I couldn't quite say the rest, and could feel my face getting messed up with tears. Mum dabbed at my eyes with a tissue and rubbed my shoulder. "What's happened?" she asked, kissing me lightly on the head.

Finally I got it out. "How come," I began,

heaving breaths, "how come I can remember this music? But I can't remember the sound of Dad's voice?"

Mum rested her head against mine. At last she said, almost whispering, "Ari, I don't know. I just don't know …" She sighed and then looked into my face. "It's almost as though he's paid you a visit, isn't it? A visit you weren't expecting, something even more real than your special photo. You've become the custodian of your father's train set. You hear and remember some music he loved to listen to. It's good, you know, to remember something about him. Even a little something, and even if it hurts."

My head ached from crying. At that moment, I missed my father very much. And no matter how hard I tried, nothing would bring the sound of his voice back to me.

TINY LIGHTS

Where was I?

In the cafe late at night, blinking my eyes. Working out where exactly I was standing. Tables two and three are *here*. The train set is over *there*.

The chairs were all up-ended on the tables; it was like finding my way through a forest of bare trees.

I blinked my eyes some more and saw the shadows of the drum kit, the piano and microphone stands. My headache was gone, but I couldn't sleep. I'd put socks on with my pyjamas, but could still feel the cold floorboards. There was a rectangle of dim light from the cafe's back window, and when my eyes focused in the almost-dark, I could see the train set on the floor beside the stage.

Friday, I worked out in my head. It's Friday morning now and we'll have to pack the train set away in time for customers tonight.

I lay on my stomach and slowly turned the power pack on. The train's tiny lights glowed into brightness and the carriages began to move along the tracks with a soft hum and clockwork clicks. I lay my head in the crook of my arm, and turned on the second power pack.

House windows were lit, tiny lights on railway platforms glowed over seats and tiny plastic people on their way to work. It made me think of my father, leaving early for work to fix a computer problem.

The third power pack switched on the goods train that ran in the opposite direction, through the tunnel and mountain, over the level crossing, and past the farms with their tiny tractors and animals.

The writing on the buildings and carriages was all in German.

"Bahnhof," I murmured softly. "Speiseraum, Schlafwagen, Trans Europ Express—"

Where was I?

On the floor at Opa's farmhouse, with the map my mum had spread like a picnic rug. Mountains higher than you can imagine. One of the longest railway tunnels in the world. An ancient city buried long ago by a volcanic eruption. Beautiful beaches and water as clear as window glass.

Where were we?

Outside our train carriage had been a black and unknown place.

You try to get some sleep, Mum had said. Tomorrow, our adventures begin.

Which was pretty much how Jamie found me later, as the first sunlight shone through the cafe window—fast asleep on the floor beside the stage, as the tiny model trains hummed and clicked around their tracks.

An e-mail, Wednesday night

Opa, I've just come back from my music lesson.

Mum could tell it hadn't gone well, but I didn't want to talk about it in the car on the way home. I complained a bit instead and she got cross with me and said she would speak with Mr Lee about things herself.

And I'm not good at telling fibs the way my friend Thomas can, so you may as well know I've been sent to my room and told not to come back out until I've stopped being a pain in the neck. Mum doesn't like complaints about music lessons and says that she and Jamie are not both working at part-time jobs and then running the cafe as well just for the fun of it. That there are bills to pay and that they want to give me a little more than just food to eat and somewhere to live.

I said, I don't care. Mum said she didn't want to hear or see me for at least twenty minutes, so go away.

Opa, Mr Lee is the most serious person I know. He never makes jokes and hardly ever smiles. He always says hello and always asks about school and how I am, and my answer is always the same—good. Good, thanks.

Only once has he asked me about the cafe and I gave the same answer, because I wasn't sure he wanted to hear about how we had a power blackout with twenty-five hungry customers waiting. Or about how scrubbing lasagne trays is my least favourite kitchen job.

So every answer from me is *Good*, and every answer from him is *Mm-hmm*. Then we get down to business, music business. He'll ask me to play this scale or that scale, he'll listen to my music homework, and sometimes play the piece back to me on his violin to show me the way he thinks it should really sound.

There's a teacher at our school, Mr Manning, and the kids he teaches all talk in the playground about how boring it is in his classroom. My class is busy and sometimes loud, and Ms Orton teaches interesting stuff, makes jokes and tells us what great kids we are. When she laughs, her jewellery rattles like Jamie's percussion instruments. I've been to Mr Manning's room on a message and it's like walking into an office, or one of those shops where no one seems to buy anything. Sometimes Mr Lee's music lesson room feels the same.

I can look out of his window and see the laneway and the back of other shops. I can see the park and the hills, cliffs and valleys. And it makes me wish I was outside somewhere else, not stuck in a room doing scales and music exercises. It's when I really miss your place, sitting out on the garden seat with that little beginner's violin, trying to copy the things you played on your concert Schuster. I miss that a lot.

Mr Lee lectured me today about having a precise technique, after I thought I'd played my Mozart homework really well. He told me I was moving around too much and not taking enough notice of the music score. I had to play it all over again.

He said, You are one of my best pupils, what has happened lately?

I wanted to say, and my grandfather was my best music teacher.

But I didn't, I just felt mad instead.

Mum and Jamie found three CDs with the orchestra you played in. One has a photo and we can see you clearly, sitting in the string section. Another of the CDs has "First violin solo: Klaus Matten". So Opa, that's proof you were a bit famous, even if you always said, Not really.

I think my twenty minutes are up now, and Mum might have calmed down. From Ari.

Mr Lee said

I didn't look forward to the next Wednesday afternoon.

Mum collected me from school as usual, and drove the short distance to the shops in town.

"I did speak to Mr Lee," she told me, parking the car in a space beside the post office arcade. "In case you thought I'd forget. Yesterday, during my lunch break."

I turned to get my violin case and music book from the back seat and climb out of the car, but Mum put one hand on my shoulder. "No, wait. Before you dash off, we need to talk. Don't pull faces at me, please."

I sat myself back in my seat. "I wasn't," I grumbled.

"All right," she sighed. "You can't do this by yourself, Ari. You need a music teacher, and when we first moved here, everyone I spoke with recommended

Mr Lee. There's some clever, wonderful stuff you've taught yourself, but you need a ... what? A guide, a mentor. And your grandfather is not around any more to do that for you. Jamie and I aren't exactly violin experts."

"But Mr Lee is boring."

"And you're being unkind. When I compare Opa's music primers and the work you bring home from Mr Lee, there's not a great difference. No hints and funny notes like Opa wrote you, sure. But what's the same? Scales, exercises, Mozart, Beethoven, lots of Bach. You need to keep learning and do something with your ... talent. There's nothing else I can call it. There's nothing else Mr Lee can call it, either."

I wasn't looking at her as she spoke. I examined my fingernails, instead.

"Ari," Mum said, "Mr Lee and I didn't spend our time grumbling about you, you know. I talked about Opa, and other things besides. And Mr Lee talked— well, put it this way: he may be someone you only see for a short time each week, but he thinks highly of you and where your talent might take you. So please, be an interested student and do your best. Can I at least hear 'Yes, Mum'?"

I sighed very loudly. "Yes, Mum. Can I go now?"

"Of course. See you in forty minutes."

So I walked along the arcade to Lee's Music

Store, in through the glass doors, past the row of shiny guitars, the brand-new drum kits and keyboards, to the studio room at the back of the shop.

"Hello," Mr Lee said, "how are you today?"

"Good," I answered softly, as everything seemed to start off the way it always did.

I did scales and warm-ups, and after a time Mr Lee said, "You're very quiet this week, Ari."

I shrugged a reply. And for the next little while, neither of us said anything. Mr Lee was using sign language—picking up his own violin, pointing with his bow at the part in the duet piece he'd set me for homework the previous week, dipping his head and raising his eyebrows to me as if to say, more expression, more volume, can we run through that again?

Finally, he put his own violin down, sat on the chair at his work desk and pointed to the second chair nearby. "Have a seat, Ari," he said, and I could hear warning bells going off in my head, a sinking feeling that I was going to be lectured by him as well.

"When we emigrated here," Mr Lee told me then, taking his glasses off and wiping the lenses with a cloth, "my parents had to work at all sorts of jobs to help our family get ahead. There was a lot of pressure put on my brothers, sisters and I to succeed at things— it was heavy going, sometimes. And I was the musical child, so of course my parents saw that as a profession—

you know, performing on the international stage, being seen in concert halls and on television. I found the idea of all that a bit much, because somewhere along the way I discovered that it wasn't performing I enjoyed, but teaching others how to play. My parents were surprised at my choice, and—who knows?—they're probably still a bit disappointed, though they don't say as much. But it was my choice with music, and here I am. Here we are."

He paused a moment, and waited for me to look up.

"Ari," he said, "in the last little while, I started to worry that you were losing interest with your music, that I had nothing more to offer you. But it was a passing thought, and it would have been like admitting failure. I like challenges—and you're a challenge. How do you like that description?"

"Mum tells me I'm a nuisance sometimes."

"And I told your mother that you are a very promising musician, and that we need to find ways to keep you developing your skills. There's a future for you in this, Ari."

He stopped talking again, and even though I was staring at my shoes, I could feel his eyes on me. When I looked up I saw his neat clothes, his shirt and tie, his combed hair, the jacket hanging on the back of his seat. "Is this the music lesson you were expecting today?" he asked, raising his eyebrows and smiling a little.

I had to shake my head. "No."

"Well ..." He glanced at his watch. "Your mother picks you up in ten minutes or so. We've enough time to squeeze in some more practice. And next week, I want you to bring along a few extra things for me. One of the primers your grandfather made for you. Maybe not one of the early ones; they were for a much younger player. One of the later books, perhaps."

Mr Lee must have seen the surprise on my face, because he smiled again. So Mum had talked about other things; I wasn't sure how I felt about that.

"Something else, too," Mr Lee added. "Some of your own music."

"What music?"

"The things you've put together yourself. Your mother told me you've been composing music since you were six years old. Why didn't I hear about this sooner?"

"It's only little bits," I explained. "It's nothing much. I haven't even written out everything I've thought of. Just some things."

"I'd very much like to see it. Why didn't you say something before?"

"I didn't want you to think ..."

"What?" he asked with a little laugh. "You didn't want me knowing that you were not just musical, but had a special talent?" Then he laughed out loud, something I'd never heard or seen him do before. "Bring that music next week, Ari Huber. Bring it, or I'll be on the doorstep of your cafe, demanding to see it."

So the following Wednesday's lesson was even more strange and different. I spent half of it sitting on the music room's second chair while Mr Lee thumbed through the last violin primer that Opa had sent me. Mr Lee nodded thoughtfully, smiled at the assortment of music, and wanted some of Opa's handwritten comments translated. He picked up his own violin and tried some of the pieces he hadn't heard of before.

"So your grandfather's had you playing jazz as well? Roland Kirk, Stephane Grappelli ... have you taught yourself all these pieces?"

"All of them."

He flicked open the first page of my own music journal. "What's this?" he asked, pointing to something in my mum's handwriting. "Ari, a number six, something about Naples."

"That's how old I was," I replied. "Mum wrote all that out, not me. I didn't know how to put it on paper properly then. It's something she heard me play, something I made up when we were on holidays in Italy."

"And how long since you've played it?"

"Maybe not since I was six."

"Well, time to dust it off. Let's hear it now."

"Now?"

"Yes, absolutely."

So I stared and frowned at the score, ran through it in my head and hoped it wouldn't sound too babyish played out loud.

I changed the last few notes, and wondered if Mr Lee noticed. He had his head turned sideways as I played, gazing as though he'd heard something outside the music room door.

"Again," he told me.

I pulled a face, but started over. It sounded better this time. Beyond my view of the violin strings, I could suddenly see and hear things that fitted with this music —the whack of a soccer ball on a Naples street, kids calling out. My mother reappearing at the doorway of a strange house, hitching up her backpack—pulling a face, the face she pulled when wine was too sweet or food too plain. I remembered the people who had given us water and lunch, but had lectured Mama about religion.

Mama. I could hear the sound of my little-child

voice, the voice that had once spoken next-to-no English.

"Again," Mr Lee repeated, but this time picked up his own violin from the desk and began to steer notes in and out of my own.

"You know something?" he asked, as we held our bows above the final note.

"What?" I asked, expecting to be told about something on my score sheet that wasn't quite right.

"There's a nice idea happening on this page," he said. "I like it. I can hear a conversation that goes with this music, and in my mind, pictures of a place. You were really only six years old when you worked this little tune out?"

I nodded.

He looked steadily at me for a moment, then nodded as well—slowly, thoughtfully. And he handed me back Opa's violin primer, but held up my own music journal. "I'd like to borrow this. May I?"

Only children

Allison had arrived early for work on Saturday.

"My major assignment," she told us, "all done. That's it for me this semester. And I had nothing else to do—so here I am."

"Wow," said Jamie, "I'm impressed. When I was at uni, I left every assignment until the last minute. What a conscientious student you are, Allison."

"Time for a bit of a celebration, then," Mum said, rummaging in the fridge for cafe leftovers and finding a portion of chocolate mud cake. And soon enough, the stereo was playing and there was talk and laughter at our dining table.

After a time I got a bit bored with uni talk and politics, and drifted away to get ready for a cafe evening. I changed into my white shirt and brocade vest and walked into the cafe to turn the lights on and get the tables set up. The phone at the counter rang;

someone wanting a table for six, and sorry they hadn't remembered to ring earlier. On my father's watch, the sun was beginning to disappear—two more hours before we opened.

I climbed up onto the stage. It was a place I sometimes explored when I knew I was alone—to tap out notes on the baby grand or the glass xylophone, to sit behind the drum kit and wonder what it would be like to make a racket and have people clap you for it.

And I allowed myself to think about Opa when he had been with the orchestra, performing on a bigger stage for an audience much larger than we would ever hope to cram into our cafe. Had he ever worried about the hundreds of people watching him play? I stood on the cafe stage and wondered about that.

I had to move the yellow chair; it had been at table six the night before. I carried it to table eight.

I'd run out of things to do. Mum had no reason to call "Show time!" because she was still in the house with Jamie and Allison. So I climbed back up onto the stage and sat at the baby grand. Allison was a good pianist and I dabbed restlessly at the keys, trying to find the sort of music she could make with her eyes closed. The times I had worked at the piano with enough concentration, I could make reasonable music. But it wasn't second nature to me like the violin was, and the baby grand made hesitant, lonely sounds. It wasn't deliberate, but gradually the notes on the piano began to sound like the music on my father's CD.

Mit Gefühl, Opa might have said. *With feeling.* And I was trying, but my father's music didn't sound so dreamlike this time. Like a tape loop, I played the bass part in circles, over and over. The notes echoed in the empty cafe as though they were being played in a cave.

"Mit Gefühl," I told myself in a whisper.

Somewhere behind me, I could hear the noise and voices in the house stop for a moment, and then begin all over—but more quietly. There were footsteps in the cafe, then a skipping jump of feet onto the stage. Allison sat herself beside me on the piano stool, and a perfumed breeze immediately swirled around my face. She always smelled of incense and fragrant oils.

"Keep playing," she said.

I edged across the stool to let her sit more comfortably, and picked up the bass progression once more. For a moment, she watched my fingers tapping out the notes, then she held her own hand above the keyboard, fingers poised. On cue, she brought her hand down to play the main melody. Suddenly it sounded exactly as it had on the CD my aunts had sent.

I stopped in surprise. "How do you know this?"

"I came out here during the week," Allison said. "A bit of a social call, a bit of discussion about this month's menu—and your mum and I, we wound up talking. About you. And she played me some music from the CD that was in those packages from Germany. So I sat out here with the stereo going, and took a little time to work this tune out properly."

"Why?"

"Because I like it. And because it means something to you. It does, doesn't it?"

"It reminds me—" I tried to explain. "I remember it from a long time ago. From when I was a little kid. I told Mum that, but I don't know if she really believed me."

"She does believe you, Ari." Allison played the melody again—first as a mystery, then in the high, chiming notes of a music box. "She showed me a photo from your bedroom, of you and your dad." She paused, then added, "This music and that photo really belong together, I saw that straight away. So do you mind if I play it some more? With your help, of course."

"You're a better player than me."

"Come on," she instructed, and soon enough, I could hear Allison adjusting her playing to mine, just as Opa might have done with the violin.

"Time for variations," she said after a few minutes. "Keep your bass chords going." And she swung the melody into a minor key, improvising notes

I hadn't heard in the original music. For a minute or two it worked, but my concentration came undone and my fingers fell onto the wrong keys.

"Don't worry about it," she said. "It's my fault for trying to show off. I thought it sounded pretty good. What about you?"

I nodded. "You're better on the piano than I'll ever be."

"And you're better on the violin than I'll ever be. This music would sound nice with your violin as accompaniment."

"Maybe it would."

"Maybe definitely! Most Fridays and Saturdays when I turn up for work I can hear you practising out in the garden. Sometimes it's hard to believe you're barely half my age."

"How old are you?" I asked.

"Me? Twenty."

"Have you got any brother or sisters?"

"No, only me. Why?"

"I just wondered, that's all."

"When I was your age," Allison said, "I used to wish that I had a brother or sister to annoy. Or talk to. A brother like you would have been okay." She smiled and gently elbowed me in the ribs. "Oh, I forgot to say—your mum showed me something else. She showed me a video."

"What video?" I asked, but knew which one almost straight away.

"Talented things come in small packages."

I groaned.

"No," Allison said, "I thought it was really great—someone I know has been on TV! You looked very cute."

I groaned again.

"And as for your mum! What a wild woman she was with those dreadlocks."

"I miss her with that hairdo, sometimes," I said more quietly, and the two of us were silent for a moment.

Allison began to play my father's music once more, this time alone and with both hands. It sounded beautiful, and my skin prickled and goosebumped.

"I do like this music," Allison said softly. "Now that I've more or less worked it out, whenever I hear it or play it, it's going to remind me of you. And of being at uni. And of this mad, special cafe. And vegetarian food …"

I nodded and smiled, but kept my own answer to myself.

It reminds me of getting on trains and leaving Opa. It reminds me of starting kindergarten in Hattorf. Most of all, it reminds me of my father and the photo in my room. It reminds me of everything.

And now, because Allison's played this music, it reminds me of here.

"Jamie wanted to call this place Cafe Fartypants," I said then, which made Allison laugh loudly.

And at that moment, Jamie and my mother strode up the hallway and into the cafe. "Ari! Allison! Show time!"

CLIMBING A HILL

"Boring," I said, before Jamie had a chance to ask. "Boring, boring."

"That good, huh? It rained all day here, too."

"We couldn't play outside at all," I said, sitting down on a kitchen chair to unlace wet school sneakers. "We were stuck on the verandah area at morning break. Grumpy Mr Manning was on duty and wouldn't even let us stand up to go and put our rubbish in the bin."

"You poor children ... There's orange and poppyseed cake over in that pastry box, would that help ease the pain?"

"At least we got to go to the library at lunchtime, to look at books and use the computers. I hate wet school days. And the inside of the bus was like Antarctica all the way home." I had a mouthful of cake by now. "When's Mum home from the bookshop?" I asked, trying not to spray crumbs across the table.

"About six o'clock. Any homework?"

"Spelling and, um, maths."

"What about music practice? Lesson day tomorrow."

I looked out of the kitchen window at my practice spot in the garden. "It's raining," I said.

"Go and practice in your room," Jamie suggested, but I pulled a face. "Go and use the cafe, then. Perfect rehearsal area. What's the practice piece this week?"

"Bach."

"He's a popular choice with Mr Lee."

"Yes," I sighed.

"You don't like Bach suddenly?"

"No, it's good music. Your timing needs to be really correct."

"Well," Jamie said, "when you've finished pigging out on cake, homework or music practice. But not out in the rain."

So I went out to the cafe, and sat on one of the stage chairs with my sheet music propped on its stand. I played my scales as the rain drummed noisily on the roof, then worked on the Bach piece as the weather quietened a little.

I'd left Jamie in the kitchen preparing things for

our dinner, but after a while he wandered out to where I was and stepped up onto the stage. "Need an accompanist?" he asked. "I recognise this piece you're playing."

"If you like," I replied and stood up, shifted myself and my music over beside the baby grand.

He studied my sheet music for a moment and experimented with the piano keys a little. "Okay, got it," he said, and we played the piece through together a couple of times. It sounded good. Then the rain got so loud on the roof we almost had to shout to hear each other. "Loud version!" Jamie called. "Let's rock out!" Which was good for a laugh, but wasn't what Mr Lee would have liked to hear.

"Had enough yet?" Jamie asked. "Sore fingers, sore shoulders?" I shook my head. "Okay," he said, "some old faves for you." And he played a couple of tunes that I knew well; tunes that we had played together before. When? It seemed like a long time ago.

Then Jamie moved on to something I didn't know, that made me stop and listen. It reminded me of the weather—soft, deep notes like faraway thunder, tinkling high notes like sprinkling rain.

"What do you want me to do?" I asked after Jamie had played it through several times.

He stopped, looked thoughtful and then said, "I guess I want you to improvise—make up your own accompaniment around the chords and melody. But bring the violin in very quietly and gently and build on the … intensity. Do you understand that?"

"I think so."

"I'll give you some words—not 'adagio' or 'brilliantismo' or anything like that—but words to make a tune with. If I was to say 'undercurrent', what would you picture in your head?"

"Um … water. Waves swirling. But quietly, not crashing."

Jamie looked pleased.

"It's like the notes Opa used to write in my music primers," I said. "Picture words and little stories about the music."

Jamie looked steadily at me for a moment, then agreed. "You're probably right. I'll tell you my last word, first. It's 'Go'. When you hear 'Go', you've twelve bars of music to do whatever you want. Give the tune a climax and a conclusion. You okay with all of that?"

"Okay."

So we played and I tried to put Jamie's list of words into music.

Wondering.

Mysterious.

Undercurrent.

Waves over sand.

Climbing a hill.

Higher, higher.

A wonderful view.

Go.

The rain was loud on the roof above us again.

When we stopped playing, I said, "My fingers and shoulders are sore now."

Jamie nodded. "For an experiment, that actually sounded very good," he said, but his face was serious.

"What is it?" I asked.

He took a breath. "I found your e-mails today. It wasn't intentional. I was downloading some holiday accommodation info. I found them by accident. I'm sorry, Ari."

I swallowed hard. "It's okay," I made myself say, "I only typed them. I didn't send them."

"You didn't?"

"There was no one to send them to."

"I read part of a couple of them and I'm sorry about that, too. But it was enough for me to see how much you miss your grandfather, and how much you looked up to him."

I didn't know what to say, and gazed outside. Grey clouds hung over the bush and the cafe garden, and rain spattered against the window glass.

"I'm sorry, Ari," Jamie said again.

"No," I repeated, "it's okay."

After a silence, I heard, "Ms Orton dropped into the bookshop the other day. Did your mum tell you?"

"No."

"For a chat as well as a book purchase. And she's heard on the grapevine that you're a musician of some ability. She asked your mum all about it. I know you don't talk about it at school, but we've lived here a while now and people will get to hear about you. Not only because Mr Lee wants you to be part of an end-of-year recital, but because music is a big part of your life. Are you that bothered that people might find out?"

"People think kids who play violins are ..."

"Weird? Some people might. I don't, your mum doesn't. The people who listened to you busking when you were eight years old certainly didn't. Did Thomas think you were weird after he heard you playing to your grandfather that time?"

"No," I had to admit.

Jamie quietly closed the piano lid, propped a hand under his chin. "So who thinks you're weird? You're not, you know—you're a clever kid who happens to be a fine musician, and you can take that skill anywhere you want. It can be as little as something special for friends and family, or as much as a career. Don't let yourself be pressured by what other people think, and don't be scared by the thought of an audience." He smiled, then reached over and patted my shoulder. "Sorry, I'll stop lecturing you now. I just want you to know how much we believe in you, even if you sometimes worry that you're not good enough. Now, before I go back to the kitchen, I've something to ask you."

"Yes?"

"That little bit of music we just worked on, it's a song. From one of the CDs your aunts sent out."

"It sounded like something I'd heard before somewhere," I said.

"Well, your mum remembered it as a favourite from long ago. She wants to work on it with me, turn it into something she and I can perform one Friday or Saturday night. I know you don't like the idea of being up on stage on cafe nights, and I know your mum has asked you before—but it's me doing the asking this time."

I realised what was going to be asked, and shifted uncomfortably. "I don't—" I began to say.

Jamie held up a hand. "It's your mum's birthday in a month, the same weekend we close for Christmas. Your aunt, uncle and cousins are travelling over from Germany to stay. I want you to think about birthdays and the sort of gifts that don't need wrapping. I'll lend you the disc that has this song. If you hear us rehearsing it over the next few weeks, have a listen to the ways we might work it."

"Did Mum want you to ask me this?"

"No, it's my very own idea, something I think you're ready for. A bridge for you to cross and a hill to climb. A special surprise for your mum on our last cafe night for the year. I'll only ask you this once, and I'll not bother you about it again if you say no. But will you think about it?"

I nodded. "I'll think about it."

Jamie nodded, too, and stood up. "The words I gave you, the ones to create music to—I'll write them down for you. It'll be a song that deserves the violin and your skill; I wouldn't be asking otherwise." He ruffled my hair. "Your mum'll be home soon, so I'd better get dinner happening. Want to come and help?"

"In a minute," I replied. But instead I sat for quite a while on the stage in our empty cafe, thinking about how to answer Jamie's question about a birthday surprise.

Then I thought about my e-mails to Opa, wondering whether to go and delete them and have them lost forever—or whether to print them out for myself and put them safely away somewhere. And if I was to write one last message to him, how would it begin?

Opa, I don't know what to do.

Above me came the steady sound of rain and,

outside the cafe window, cloud mist moved among the trees beyond our garden.

A wonderful view.

As I kept gazing, the music began to find its way into my head—there as easily as a daydream.

THE FRIDAY BOY

The black Saab had pulled up across the road.

I could see the mother and her boy seated in the front as always, sometimes perfectly still, sometimes shifting in their seats and talking to each other. The boy spent a long time looking down—at a book, a computer game?

They'd been parked out there for ages today. I'd done my violin practice and come inside. I'd set the tables, folded napkins and checked the iced water supply. Mum had drawn up the chalkboard menu and set it on the counter top. I'd gotten out of washing lettuce leaves in the cafe kitchen, but had been sent off in search of a replacement globe for the piano light. And I'd moved the yellow chair from table eleven to table one.

By now, it was nearly sunset and the Friday boy was still with his mother in the car across the road, waiting for his father to show.

My violin case and music book were on the arrival lounge where I'd dumped them earlier, and because there was nothing else to do, I got the violin back out and walked over to sit on the edge of the stage. I plucked a few tunes out, pizzicato, half-expecting Mum to step out of the kitchen and give me another list of things that needed doing. But the cafe's front door swung open instead. We'd had a drinks delivery earlier and I'd forgotten to lock the door afterwards.

The boy from the black Saab was inside and he headed towards the counter. It took him a moment to see me sitting over at the stage and I could tell it was unexpected; he looked surprised.

I still had the violin up next to my ear. "We're closed," I said, taking the violin back to its case then walking over to where he stood. "We open at six-thirty for dinner."

"I just wanted a can of drink," the Friday boy said.

"We're a restaurant," I explained, and right at that moment the chainsaw buzz of the food processor came from the kitchen. Mum, Jamie and Allison began to shout a conversation above the racket. "We're a restaurant," I repeated, "we don't sell takeaway." And I suddenly felt bad-mannered for saying so.

The boy looked at me. "My dad's late. He's

nearly always late. Once he even forgot and didn't turn up at all. Sitting out there in the car now is driving me crazy."

He looked a bit lost and unsure of what to do or say next. I was unsure too. I could see his mother still sitting out in her car and felt a bit sorry for them both.

"I just wanted, you know, a can of drink. Coke or lemonade or something." The boy was about my age and height, with hair the colour of rust. He wore expensive label clothes and he'd been sitting out there in a nice car. And his dad was late.

Mum had heard our voices and popped her head out the cafe kitchen door. "Hello," she said to the boy, "are you a friend of Ari's?"

I shook my head and asked about selling drinks. She shrugged then said, "Not usually, but this time it's okay," before stepping back into the kitchen. The food processor started buzzing again.

"We've got mineral water," I told the boy. "I can sell you a bottle of that. What about your mum?"

He looked grateful, and held out some coins. "That'd be great. Thanks."

I was fishing around in the drinks fridge behind the counter when he said, "So you're the one who plays violin. I've heard you when I've waited out the front before."

"Practising, probably. Out in the backyard. I've seen you before, too. Every second Friday."

"That's when I go to stay with my dad. Every second weekend. We wait out the front here because it's halfway between where my parents live."

"What school do you go to?"

"St Dominic's."

"I go to Mount Street Public."

The Friday boy looked around the cafe. "Do you live here? What about the stage, those instruments? Whose are they?"

He looked impressed when I told him about the cafe and the music. "Sounds like cool fun. Do you play on stage, too?"

"No."

"But I've heard you playing, you're pretty good. Better than me, I think."

"You play music, too?"

"Violin. Grade four. I learn at school."

"I'm grade five," I told him. "I started playing when I was three, my grandfather taught me. But I have lessons in town now. Wednesdays at Lee's Music."

We stared at each other for a moment. Then the boy said, "There's probably things we both know how to play. Maybe next time we can play some music together while I'm waiting for my dad. It'd sure beat sitting in the car."

I shrugged. "Yeah, that'd be good." And felt surprised to have said so. I realised I didn't even know his name, and added, "I'm Ari."

"I'm Felix."

"Felix!" I repeated, and laughed with recognition. From the look on his face, he must have thought I was laughing at him. So I had to explain that it was a name I knew from long ago—when? And I remembered sitting in darkness, waiting for a train that hadn't arrived, and the people with the bookshop who gave Mum and me a bed for the night. And photos of grandchildren. Which one was the naughtiest? I'd asked. *Felix*.

"We sent them postcards," I said, "to say thank you. And on my postcard, I wrote that I'd like to meet the naughtiest grandchild one day."

I wasn't sure what Felix thought of my story, but he listened quietly and then said, "I've never met anyone else with my first name."

"Me either."

"So did you ever meet the other Felix?"

"Never. And the people we met when we travelled—it'd be just the once, then never again."

Felix glanced out to where his mother's car was. "I'd better go, Mum's not in a good mood. Only because of my dad, she's nice the rest of the time." He looked around the cafe again. "It'd be great to come here for the food and music some time. I'll ask Mum. Or Dad. And the next Friday I'm here," he added, "I'll bring my violin. See you."

"See you," I replied. And he walked out, letting the cafe door click shut behind him. I watched him cross the road, get into the black Saab and begin talking with his mother.

"Have you run out of things to do?" came my own mum's voice. She was leaning on the glass-topped counter.

"Yes," I had to admit. "But guess what?"

She nodded and smiled. "I know. We weren't exactly eavesdropping on you in there, but we heard the conversation. A nice coincidence, wasn't it? Ari—"

"Yes?"

"Next time Felix is out the front in his mother's car waiting, violin or not, go and invite him inside. If you can make a friend, then something good has come out of a coincidence. Especially if he likes playing music as much as you. Now," she pointed, "go and put your violin and music things away. We need you in the kitchen."

I groaned, picturing a sink full of salad greens to be washed. But no.

"Come and keep us company," Mum said instead.

A THOUGHT, NOT AN E-MAIL

It took a while, Opa, but I finally found a photo of you and me that I always really liked, right from the time it was taken.

We were in the field behind the house and you were sitting on that rickety green garden seat. I was standing beside you. We were both playing music, except I can't remember what. And we didn't even know she had the camera out, but Mum took our picture. The telephoto lens made it look as though she was right under our noses, though actually she wasn't. She was way over beside the house.

So the photo is really our faces only, and we're so close our cheeks are almost touching—like I was trying to give you a hug as well as hold my violin and the bow.

And your eyes are closed; you're smiling as though there's a good dream happening in your head.

But me, my eyes are open and I'm concentrating so hard on my playing it looks as though I'm frowning. Just like in the video, when Mum and I busked at the markets all that time ago.

Aunty Monika, Uncle Tim, Anya and Björn arrive tomorrow. Even though they're hiring a car to go travelling with, we're still waking up before dawn to drive down to the city and meet them at the airport. It'll be good to have them here, and there's lots to show them. I still wish every day and every week that you'd been able to come and visit, too.

I've made up my mind, Opa. It's about playing music.

On Saturday, it'll be Mum's birthday. She'll be thirty-five, you know, and she's not thrilled about it. She keeps saying, I still feel twenty-five in my head. Tell me this is not happening, someone!

And she found this song, an old favourite of hers. It's the one she wants to finish Saturday night's cafe show with. Because after that, we're closed for Christmas and New Year. Four more school days, then we travel north with our guests, to show them our favourite beaches and rainforests.

The song is about travelling. Jamie lent me the CD to listen to and think about, because the way he wants the song performed will give it a whole instrumental section at the end. He asked me to work out something for the violin that might fit, as a birthday surprise for Mum. When she was in town one afternoon, Jamie and I sat out in the cafe with our instruments and worked on it for a while. And it sounded pretty good.

But I wanted to work out Mum's birthday surprise properly, so I began writing my ideas onto a music score sheet. I've worked on my surprise music every day for nearly two weeks now, even at school when Ms Orton wasn't looking. I had a couple of score sheets tucked away in my activity folder along with the usual maths and spelling work. So if an idea came into my head, I was able to write it out straight away.

Whenever Mum and Jamie have been rehearsing a song—trying different ways of singing it, trying different combinations of instruments—when they've been practising and practising, and finally they have it the way they want it to be—they nearly always say, "I think we've got this one nailed."

That's how it is for me now, Opa. I've really worked on this music. I've changed bits around. I've practised and practised.

I think I've got it nailed.

In the photo of you and me, I'm about six. That's the age of Mr Lee's youngest pupil, a six year old. She goes to my school, and I didn't even know before that she learned music. Mr Lee's oldest pupil is seventeen. I know all his other pupils now.

I remember you telling me once that even adults could be a nightmare when it came to rehearsing a piece of music, and the first practice by Mr Lee's string ensemble was a bit the same. We made mistakes, we got the giggles and Mr Lee did a great job of being patient. But after three or four practice sessions, our end-of-year concert pieces are starting to sound pretty good. It's been fun, and I hadn't expected that.

Mr Lee told me, You've made an important decision, Ari. It's really great that you're going to be part of this.

But before all that comes Mum's birthday surprise. And it's being up on the cafe stage that worries me.

After Jamie and I first tried out Mum's song, I sat in the cafe by myself to think for a while. And out of everything I had to work out answers to, it was Thomas I was suddenly thinking about, how Thomas isn't scared of anything. He's not scared of getting into trouble at school, or of horror movies or of looking silly when he dances at school discos. But Thomas *is* scared of heights. When I took him to the lookout, he wouldn't go near the edge to see the view.

So I stood on the stage and tried to think of it as

the lookout. I looked down at the tables and empty chairs as though they were the view from somewhere high. Then I imagined the cafe full of people, all of them watching me. And I listed the things I was worried about ... Breaking a string. Playing music in the wrong key. Making a mistake in front of an audience. Having people think that a kid with a violin must be weird. Except I'm not so worried about that last bit any more.

I bought a frame for the photo that I found of us. It's a good photo, Opa, because when I look at my own face, I can see that it's almost the beginning of everything I've learned so far about music. And when I look at your face, I know what sort of musician I want to be.

So I've made up my mind about music, and that means I've decided about being on stage as well. I just hope I can close my eyes and smile as I play, the way you used to. I don't want to be staring and frowning, not on Mum's birthday.

ARRIVING

Mum held up a small page of paper.

I could see it from where I sat in the back of the station wagon, and for a tiny moment, it could have been the other side of the world: the back of Opa's car as he had driven us to the airport, the paper with names and addresses that Mum had held up to reassure Opa we would have friends to meet us and places to stay.

The sound of his voice was still in my head. Such a long way ... Such a big trip for a small boy.

This time, as Mum held up the piece of paper she was tapping keys on her mobile phone and then listening to a recorded message about flight arrivals. Jamie steered the car along the curves and climbs of the highway, as the first daytime colour showed in the sky above ridges and treetops.

Mum nodded as she clicked her mobile off.

"On time," she told us. "Their flight's still on schedule."

Mum, Jamie and I waited for what seemed like ages. Then my aunt, uncle and cousins came through the automatic doors and down the arrival ramp with their trolley of luggage, and we were all calling out to each other. Amid the hugs and kisses and greetings, Uncle Tim took something off the luggage trolley and passed it to me.

"This should now be yours," he told me in English. It was the case that held Opa's concert violin. In German, my uncle added, It needs to be cared for and played, not still and gathering dust.

I was surprised into silence and couldn't reply straight away.

"Danke," was all I could finally manage. *Thanks.*

Outside in the back of the car, with my cousin next to me, I nursed the violin case as though it were a baby.

Björn was dressed for a day at the beach. He wore a pair of reflector sunglasses bought duty-free during the stopover in Bangkok, and it was impossible to see his eyes or work out who he might be looking at. At the airport, he'd been weirdly quiet, but once settled in the back of the hire car, he began talking non-stop. Much like my mum and aunt were doing in the front seat.

How much English do you know? I asked Björn.

He held up a finger and thumb and spaced them a little apart. "So viel," he answered. *This much.*

The car smelled plastic and new, very different to our station wagon, which smelled of dust and usually had a stray vegetable or empty juice bottle rolling around under the seat. I felt a bit embarrassed about Uncle Tim and Anya riding ahead of us in the station wagon; Anya would be used to her father's flash Audi, to airconditioning, leather seats and a digital stereo.

I heard Mum joking with Aunty Monika about her city driving skills, saying that living at the cafe had turned her into a bit of a country bumpkin. So apologies for not being in the correct turning lane, and sorry about the guy in the hatchback behind us tooting his horn and probably swearing as well.

Between asking me about school and telling me about his soccer team's great season, Björn was looking all around at what we passed. In the middle of three driving lanes, heavy trucks, traffic lights and advertising billboards, he asked, "Na, wo sind denn nun die Kangeruhs?" *So where are the kangaroos, then?*

There were groans from the front seat.

Always the comedian, Aunty Monika said.

They're at the beach, my mother replied.

I looked at Björn's bright beach shirt and shorts and decided to risk a scolding from Mum. Your legs are whiter than my willy, I told him.

He laughed, and gave me a punch in the arm.

Of course Mum's radar ears were working. "Ari!" Her eyes glared at me from the rear-view mirror. "Maybe we should have put all you males in Jamie's car. Then Anya could have ridden with us instead and the conversation might be a bit more intelligent."

Björn and I were having fits of giggles. "Sorry, Mum," I managed to say, "but his legs are really white. Whiter than—"

Mum held a hand up. "Enough! I don't wish to know!"

"—this car."

Mum and Aunty Monika traded looks and shook their heads. "Boys ..." Mum said. "Who'd have them?"

Björn and I traded grins. And I felt pleased then, really pleased to have my relatives all here to visit.

Björn kept asking questions. How far from town was our place? What was on TV, did I have a soccer ball, was school still on?

Four more days of it, I told him. Maybe you can come along one day. I'll ask Ms Orton. You can be my show-and-tell.

I'd already asked Thomas if I could borrow the bike his older brother no longer rode.

There's a good place we can take bikes, I told

Björn. A bush track that goes to a lookout. A quiet road that leads to a pine forest, just like the one near Opa's.

We've got babies, Björn announced to everyone in the car. Two of Opa's goats had kids and we watched them all being born. One had a girl, the other had twins. A boy and a girl. I called the boy Ari.

Thanks a lot! I said, not quite laughing at the joke.

Björn watched me for a moment, then reached across and put his hand on my shoulder. He was a year younger than me, but the way he did this made him seem almost a grown-up.

It was my idea about bringing the violin, he said. I thought you were the person who should be playing it and looking after it. Mum and Dad and Anya all agreed. Opa would have, too. And there's a couple of books and stuff like strings and resin blocks all packed into our bags for you.

He looked at me, waiting for a reply, and I was aware of my mum and Aunty Monika waiting for me to say something as well.

So I nodded slowly and replied, "Danke. Ich bin froh sie zu haben." *Thank you. I'm glad to have them.*

And I really meant it.

TWELVE BARS

My mother's voice was whisper-soft.

It was a song for double bass and glass xylophone only, a song she had sung before and one I knew well. If Thomas had been here tonight, he might have gone, *Yeeuk, a lurrve song*. But to me, the music was perfect; it made all the cafe customers sit very still and quiet at their tables. I was over on the arrival lounge with Björn and the song had made him go very still and quiet, too. Which meant it was working better than a magic spell.

He snapped out of his little daydream as Mum stepped back from the microphone and Ben let a few last notes ripple from the double bass. And the cafe went from silence to racket as the customers clapped and called out, as everyone on stage—Mum, Jamie, Allison, Ben—did their Thank you, Goodnight bows and smiles. It always happened this way at the end of a night's music, that the quiet last song was never really the end of the show.

"Thank you," Mum said, stepping back to the microphone. "We're glad not to have put you all to sleep just yet. Now ..." And she walked to the back of the stage to pluck the guitar from its stand.

I was goosebumpy, watching Mum's every move, making sure that she was about to play the right song. Opa's violin case was at my feet and I reached down to click it open.

"Does the guitar match the cocktail frock?" Mum asked the audience, and began to have a conversation with the people at table four. "Maybe it should be a folk singer's woolly jumper and a pair of jeans, yes?"

She paused and smiled. "This has been our second year of food and music at the Mayfair Cafe. To our regulars, thank you for always returning. It makes us and our bank manager happy people. If tonight has been your first visit to this slightly mad place—"There was laughter and a few cheers, "—then we hope to feed and entertain you some more in the New Year. So, to finish—a song I taught myself to play, long ago and far away." And she gave the guitar a test strum, repositioned the instrument microphone a little.

I was on my feet.

"Viel Glück," Björn whispered. *Good luck.*

The audience had hushed as Mum prepared to play, but began to whisper and talk as I stepped between their tables and chairs, the violin and bow in one hand: the boy who usually showed them to their tables and who cleared away their empty plates was doing something unexpected.

I climbed up onto the stage beside Mum and it took her completely by surprise. "Hello," she said in a quiet, puzzled voice. I could tell she wanted to ask, Okay, what's happening? as she looked around at Jamie, Allison and Ben for answers. But all they did was smile, shrug and wear silly expressions.

"Twelve bars," I told her softly when she looked back to me. "I need twelve bars of music at the end of the song."

She nodded a slow reply, blinked her eyes, stood herself quite still and looked down for a moment.

The stage light was warm on my face. I tried to stand just as still, breathing slowly and staring out into the cafe's shadows and dark. I could see Björn's face in the distance on the arrival lounge, my uncle, aunt and cousin Anya at the table they had chosen for themselves.

Mum lifted her face to the microphone. "So, to finish—a song from my past." She glanced and nodded in my direction. "A song from *our* past. Maybe about a mother and her boy who once went travelling, who met all kinds of people along the way. And with wonderful good fortune, found themselves one day in this cafe, in a room full of friends." She turned back to me. "Okay?" she whispered.

I nodded a reply, once.

And she began to play. I lifted the violin to my chin and made myself focus on fingers, strings and bow as the song carried all of us forward. I followed the map of notes and words as Mum sang into the cafe's darkness.

Wondering.

Mysterious.

Undercurrent.

Waves over sand.

Climbing a hill.

Higher, higher.

A wonderful view.

Go.

There was another map of things in my head that I could see and feel and remember—my father, who had danced his baby boy around a room to his favourite music. The airconditioned cool inside a train carriage, the silence of railway stations late at night. Voices speaking other languages, the crowds in unfamiliar streets, my hair being ruffled by strangers.

The rush along an airport tarmac, the sudden giddy lift off the ground, the clunk somewhere beneath my feet of plane wheels folding away. And buildings and trees falling into the distance, stripes of road and patches of water and green; everything growing smaller and fading to a blur. My nose pressed against a window to say goodbye to Opa, and then his face and shape left far behind as well.

Leaving and arriving. If I had chosen to say no to playing at the Saturday markets, if we had even chosen to play our music on a different piece of footpath, Mum and I might never have met Jamie. The cafe would still be locked and empty, instead of being home for me and my family.

All of this I'd thought about—in my classroom at school, in the afternoon shade of the cafe garden or the night-still of my bedroom. It had all become the black dots, circles and lines on my music score paper. I remembered everything.

And I brought the violin bow slowly to a stop, let the final high E note dangle in the space somewhere in front of me. It was a moment long enough for me to know that I hadn't closed my eyes and smiled to play, the way I had wanted. That I'd watched every movement of my fingers and the bow, that my foot had tapped all the way along like a metronome.

It was only tiny, that moment of silence.

"Fabulous, Ari," I heard Jamie whisper somewhere nearby. "Fabulous, fabulous," before the cafe was filled with another racket of clapping and cheers.

And my mum, who was never lost for something to say, could only turn and stare at me. It was good to see the surprise on her face.

"Alles Gute zum Geburstag, Mama," I said to her. *Happy birthday.*

She began to smile, so much that I had the awful thought she might be about to plant sloppy kisses on my face in front of everyone. But instead she reached out, took my hand and held it very firmly. I remembered the audience then, nodded my head once to say thank you, and let myself smile, at least as much as Mum was still doing.

Some of the customers had stood up to clap. I could see Björn using the arrival lounge as a trampoline and could certainly hear his voice. I could see the customers who were regulars, the ones who always said, Hi Ari, how are you? when they arrived each time. And the faces I didn't recognise, the people who heard the accent in my voice and might ask, And where are you from?

I wanted to imagine another customer— who arrived late, who wore a brocade vest and carried a travel bag, who called out, "Schön gespielt, Ari!" *Nicely played.*

Except that it was Uncle Tim who called it out this time, and the moment he managed to distract me was when Mum planted a sneaky kiss on the top of my head. "Thank you, Ari," she said in my ear. "That was very special."

Allison and Ben were tinkling little runs of notes on keys and strings. Jamie had his xylophone mallets in one hand and his other hand on Mum's shoulder. "I don't think," he said above the noise from the audience, "that we can start our holidays just yet. What should we play next?"

I let go of Mum's hand and tucked the violin back under my chin, waiting for Jamie's count and the music to start.

My grandfather's violin, it fitted like comfortable clothing.

Thank you

Johannes, a promising violinist

Ingrid & Frank, their friends and families, for giving life to an idea (and for help with the translations)

Everyone near and dear, for encouragement and support above and beyond the call of duty

In fond remembrance of the Cafe Boom-Boom—fine food and fabulous music!